WRATH OF RED DOG

He had been out for awhile; he tried to sit up, but couldn't. The sun was blinding in his black eyes.

A shadow came between him and the sun. He saw the Apache standing over him. Red Dog smelled as bad as the cattle.

"I killed your friends," the Apache said with a cheerful leer. "It was pretty easy."

Raider's mouth was dry. "Why didn't you just kill me?"

Red Dog laughed. Raider tried to see if the Indian had others with him, but found that he could not turn his head. He was staked down with rawhide, his arms and legs spread eagle. His head had been fixed as well, not to mention the wet rawhide around his neck.

Red Dog touched Raider's bonds. "Wet rawhide shrinks down fast," the Indian said. "It cuts into your wrists and ankles. Also your head and neck. Sometimes it doesn't shrink far enough. So you don't die of strangling. You die slower. The thing is, will you strangle, or will you just die from the heat?"

Other books in the *Raider* series by
J. D. HARDIN

RAIDER

SINS OF THE GUNSLINGER

J.D. HARDIN

BERKLEY BOOKS, NEW YORK

SINS OF THE GUNSLINGER

A Berkley Book/published by arrangement with
the author

PRINTING HISTORY
Berkley editon/January 1989

ISBN: 0-425-11315-9

A BERKLEY BOOK ® TM 757,375
Berkley Books are published by the Berkley Publishing Group,
200 Madison Avenue, New York, NY 10016
The name "BERKLEY" and the "B" logo
are trademarks belonging to the Berkley Publishing Corporation.

PRINTED IN THE UNITED STATES OF AMERICA

10 9 8 7 6 5 4 3 2 1

This book is dedicated to Michael DeSimone and Marvin Guten, for lending a hand early on and teaching me a lot of things I needed to know.

CHAPTER ONE

The grey gelding's hooves made soft, crunching sounds in the layer of thin snow and brittle frost that covered the rolling plain. Raider's black eyes stared straight ahead into the night, not sure if he was looking at the horizon or the dipping brim of his black Stetson. It had been a cold spring, lasting well into the middle of June. The big Pinkerton agent from Arkansas hoped like hell that the last snow had fallen. His task would be a damned sight easier if things warmed up.

Raider shifted in the saddle, trying to work out the pain in his lower back. He was dressed for the weather—a thick, shearling jacket, longjohns under his flannel shirt and denim pants, an extra pair of socks that made his Justin boots fit tighter. He was still damned cold.

But there was no time to stop and build a fire. He had to finish his job. The sheriff in Helena had hired him to chase one Johnson Selks, a bad egg of long standing in Montana, dating back to the days when Helena was called Last Chance Gulch. As the sheriff explained it to Raider, Selks just couldn't get used to Helena trying to be a respectable town. The citizenry had attempted time and again to reform Selks, but he could not seem to get a handle on being decent.

Selks walked a road of crime until finally he shot a man. That had been the end of the town's patience. Unfortunately, at the time of the shooting, the sheriff had been in Butte on business and Selks had escaped. When the lawman returned, the mayor urged him to go after the outlaw. The sheriff replied that he did not want to leave his town unguarded again, so he sought to employ the famous Pinkerton agency, which in turn assigned Raider to the case.

As he plodded on into the cold night, Raider kept telling

himself that the sheriff had simply not wanted to go after Selks. He didn't really care, as long as Selks was gone. More than one man had been shot in Helena and the small-town lawman figured a man like Selks would find a bullet somewhere down the road. He couldn't care less about catching him.

But respectability had its share of entanglements, among them being the pressure of the citizens' committee. Raider had seen it before: a few righteous souls brought to bear their version of right and wrong and imposed it on the rest of the community. The big man from Arkansas figured all towns needed those types—the watchdogs of propriety—but he was sure as hell glad he didn't have to live with them.

The grey snorted and shuddered. Raider climbed down and pulled a half-full feed bag from his saddlebag. He fixed the bag over the grey's ears and started walking. It felt good to stretch his legs. Most of the soreness was gone from his body. The unfortunate fall hadn't killed him. At least he could be thankful for that.

Raider drew in a cold breath, exhaling it with disgust. He hated himself for what had happened at Blackfoot Bend. He had ridden in looking for Selks, half-expecting the old outpost to be deserted. Instead he had found a general store and a livery, both of which survived from business brought in by the cattlemen of eastern Montana.

The general store seemed to be thriving. There was food, whiskey, a bathtub, supplies, and a Kiowa whore who worked upstairs. Raider had fully intended to stop at whiskey, but after a few shots of red-eye, he sought the diversion of the Kiowa woman.

She was big, rough-looking. Long, coarse hair, thick lips, scars on her body from Lord knew what. Round thighs, big floppy breasts. Raider hadn't even bothered to undress. She had worked the buttons of his pants, pretending excitement, reaching for his thick member.

Her act turned to the real thing when she gripped his cock and realized its size. She leaned back on the bed, eagerly spreading her thick thighs. He could see her patchy bush, the flash of moistness, the parting of her labia.

His need was heightened by the long hours of trailing his

quarry, nights spent of sleeping in the saddle, the sparseness of food and water. He fell on top of her and prodded her crevice with the head of his cock. She arched her back and accepted him, writhing until they were both covered with sweat . . .

Raider tried to stop himself from dwelling on it, but he could not get the events that had followed out of his mind.

He had undressed after the first time and stayed the night with her. She wanted it again toward morning, waking him by fondling his prick. He had rolled over and impaled her, working his hips until they had reached their climaxes. Raider had intended to go back to sleep but a sound from the street caught his ears. He rose and looked out the window, only to see a man who might have been Johnson Selks tying his horse to the front porch of the general store. Raider had reached back for his pants, slipping them on in a hurry. He eased open the window and stepped out onto the porch roof.

He could still hear the words they had spoken.

"Selks!" he had cried.

The man in the duster had stepped back, raising his hands. "Whoa, big man," he said, looking up. "Don't burn me. I ain't got no truck with you."

Raider aimed for the middle of the man's chest with the Winchester. "Are you Johnson Selks, from Helena?"

The sun-wrinkled face had contorted into suspicion. "Who might be lookin' for me?"

"Pinkerton agency, on behalf of the Helena sheriff. Now lay down flat on the ground, belly down. Keep them hands up or I'll drop you."

But Selks had been too quick and too smart. He lunged to his right, slapping his mount on the flank, shouting at the top of his voice. The horse, a strong bay mare, reared and pulled back, exerting pressure on the beam that held up the center of the porch roof.

Raider felt the post going out from under him. The roof collapsed, sending him sliding downward, cascading straight into the watering trough below. Selks swung into the saddle and lit out, going southeast. If Raider had not been knocked unconscious from the fall, he might have risen and fired a couple shots from the Winchester. But as it stood, he had given Selks a half-hour head start, a fact that still grated on him like a raw blister.

The woman had distracted him.

He told himself to shut up. It hadn't been the woman at all. It had been his own foolishness, his lack of caution. It was one thing to do something stupid, it was another to blame somebody else when it was your own fault. If there was one sin under God's heavens, it was blaming somebody else for your mistakes.

Why in hell had he stepped out on that roof?

He was showing off. For the woman. For himself. He wanted Selks to see who he was dealing with. But now the Montana bad man probably figured Raider was some greenhorn, certainly no one to fear.

The thought made the big Pinkerton bristle. He hated living with mistakes. And if Selks escaped . . . maybe he would just have to retire and go back to Arkansas.

He kept leading the gelding into the night. He would have to stop and give both of them a rest. Maybe at dawn. Until then, there was nothing to do but keep on in the stubborn pursuit of duty.

His black eyes watched the stars until the clouds blew in. Raider stiffened, thinking more snow was on the way. But then he realized that the air had actually gotten warmer.

"Rain. Damn it all."

A spring storm. Just what he needed to make it worse. It drenched him and made dark puddles beneath his feet.

Raider thought over his night with the Kiowa woman and his unsuccessful run-in with Selks once again. He decided to blame her for half his troubles, even if he had behaved stupidly, too. Considering how distracting they were, he decided to swear off women. Then he saw lights glowing in the distance.

Raider clomped up the rickety wooden steps, hesitating in the rain. He didn't know where the hell he was or what kind of men he was going to meet on the other side of the door. Before he could second guess himself, the door swung open and a skinny, bald-headed man glared out at him. The man chewed a corncob pipe between his brown lips.

Suddenly the skinny man smiled. "Get on in here, stranger. Before your drowned yourself out there."

Raider went into the slapdash dwelling, easing through the shadows into a circle of lantern glow.

Two men were seated by a potbellied stove. The bald man with the corncob pipe rejoined them, sitting down to turn an ear to a large, grey-haired man. Another man who dressed like an undertaker also focused his attention on the bigger man.

Raider just stood, listening to him talk.

"So there I was," continued the grey-haired man, "trapped on all sides by Blackfoot braves. They was above me on the mountain and below me on the trail. Blackfoots is mean, don't you know."

The undertaker bellowed with a loud voice for a small man. "Had to ship most of 'em up t' Canada."

Corncob pipe nodded in agreement. "Back then, I'da took my chances with the Kiowa or the Flathead before I'd tangle with a Blackfoot."

Grey-hair paused, rubbing his belly. "That's no idle truth."

Undertaker was still hanging on the story. "So what happened?"

Grey-hair looked at his friend with grave seriousness. "Them damned Blackfoots . . ."

"Yeah?"

"Why, they killed me, dang it!"

Raider laughed first. It was the oldest story west of the Mississippi, but the look on the undertaker's face was funny enough to give anyone a guffaw. The others laughed with him, except for the undertaker who realized the joke was at his expense. He did the smart thing, however, and remained quiet.

When the laughter was over, all eyes turned to Raider.

The man with the corncob regarded him without caution. "So, stranger, can I offer you a cup o' coffee or some corn whiskey?"

Raider nodded gratefully. "Yes sir, you can offer me both if you like."

Corncob gave him a chair. Raider sat by the stove, raising his hands to the warmth. When the feeling came back into his fingers, he unbuttoned his coat, standing to take it off. The grey-haired man's eyes bulged at the sight of Raider's Colt .45 Peacemaker, riding low on his leg gunslinger-style. Raider hung the shearling coat on the back of the chair and sat down again.

"Just put that red-eye in with the coffee," he called to the balding man.

Undertaker, who had also caught sight of the Colt, was gaping without a word on his lips.

Grey-hair decided to test the waters. "Have to admire a man who sweetens his coffee with corn squeezin's."

Raider knew he had to put things at ease in a hurry. "Been doin' it since I was a pup back in Arkansas."

"That where you hail from?"

Smoke rolled from the corncob as the balding man brought Raider a steaming tin cup. "Jubal, give this man a chance to thaw out before you go jawin' him t' death. Here, big man. Take the chill off."

Raider sipped the hot liquid, feeling the life flow back into him. "Di'n't know there was a settlement in this part o' Montana."

"Maybe 'cause this is South Dakota," the corncob man replied. "You're in what some call Rapid City, mister."

Raider nodded. "Reckon I lose track out there sometimes."

Undertaker's voice came out in a prolonged squeak. "That sure is a big gun on your hip, mister. You on the run?"

Raider shot him a sidelong glare. "Yeah, I'm, runnin'. But not away from somebody. I'm after a man."

"Bounty hunter?" Grey-hair asked. "Or just a grudge?"

Corncob tapped out his pipe. "Will you two quit badgerin' this boy. Don't pay them no mind, sir. They're idlers."

Both men took exception to their friend's slight, but they were over it quickly enough to make Raider think the slight had been issued before.

"You're the slacker!" Undertaker declared.

Grey-hair echoed the sentiment, adding: "An' don't forget it!"

"Besides," Undertaker declared, "you're actin' so smart like you know who this stranger is."

Corncob turned squarely and regarded the big Pinkerton. "I reckon I do know who he is."

Raider had to smile at the old man. "Tell me then, pardner. Who am I?"

A glint in the man's mud-brown eyes. "You're chasin' a boy name o' Johnson."

Raider leaned forward. "How you know that?"

"You gotta be the Pinkerton on his trail."

Raider came up out of his chair, drawing his Colt. "You better tell me quick how you know that, citizen."

Grey-hair and Undertaker flinched, but the pipe remained steady in the other man's hand. "You ain't gonna shoot me. I ain't done nothin' wrong."

"Was Johnson through here?"

Corncob nodded. "This mornin'. Tol' me his name, but di'n't tell me no other. I figured the rest myself."

"No such thing!" Undertaker declared.

"We didn't see no Johnson through here!" Grey-hair echoed.

Raider pointed a finger at both of them. "Shut-up! Now."

"You two were in town," Corncob replied. "He had that look, like he was thinkin' o' robbin' me. I figgered somebody was on his trail, 'cause he lit out purty fast."

Raider eased back, holstering the Colt. "He say which way he was goin'?"

"Rode east. Ain't but two things east o' here. The Missouri River and Sioux Falls. And a lot o' country in between."

Raider grimaced at the old leprechaun. "You got a good eye, sir. How you know I was a Pinkerton?"

Corncob shrugged. "I couldn't forget them black eyes in a hundred years."

Raider's coal-tar irises glinted in the lantern light. "That so?"

"Yes, I reckon this might be cheatin', but you was through here 'bout five years ago with your pardner. A dandy sort, weren't he?"

Raider nodded. "Yep, that he was. Went back east an' married up on me. Gotta work by my lonesome now. Dog me if I remember bein' through here, though. Nothin' looks familiar."

"It ain't the kinda place you want t' remember," the host replied.

Undertaker stood up suddenly. "I gotta go."

He hurried out without looking back.

Grey-hair laughed. "What's wrong with him?"

"Prob'ly pissed his pants when the Pinkerton here brought out his hog leg. I thought I heard runnin' water."

They all laughed again.

Raider sighed after a while, staring at the dark window of the wooden structure. Hard rain pelted the glass, reminding him that he had to get back on the trail of Johnson Selks. He drained the last of the coffee from the tin cup. The man with the corncob pipe offered him a refill.

Raider shook his head. "One thing you can help me with."

"Go ahead."

"Any chance o' gettin' a fresh mount this time o' night?"

Corncob looked doubtful.

Raider reached into his pants pocket, taking out five gold pieces.

Corncob's eyes widened at the sight of the double eagles.

"I'll pay extra an' offer my nag in trade," Raider said. "I'll even kick in an extra two bucks if you feed me an' give me a place t' sleep for a couple a hours."

Corncob nodded. "Done."

Raider flipped him one coin, which he promptly caught. "You get the rest when my horse is ready. Take the saddle out front. And don't steal nothin' from the saddlebags."

Corncob just nodded, rising slowly out of the chair. "How long you want t' sleep?"

"An hour an' half again."

"In back there, you'll find a place. Don't need t' pay extra. The hundred'll cover it all."

He held up the gold piece, examining it closely.

Raider had to smile. "You're a cool creek, old-timer. You didn't even blink when I pulled my gun."

Corncob snapped his fingers.

Raider looked over his shoulder to see an older woman easing from the shadows with a scatter gun.

"My wife," the man said calmly. "She woulda shot you if I had said the word. Had the drop on you. Had it on that Johnson feller, too."

"You coulda saved me a lot o' trouble if you'da shot 'im," Raider offered.

They all enjoyed a good laugh for a couple of seconds, including the man's wife. She put down her shotgun and went to fix Raider's bed. The big man didn't even think about the chances of finding a woman in Rapid City. He had sworn off for good, at least until after he caught Jackson Selks.

CHAPTER TWO

William Wagner, assistant director of the Pinkerton National Detective Agency, sat at his desk behind a pile of case folders that had been read and closed that very day. Ordinarily, Wagner would have felt proud of himself for having accomplished so much in one working day, but the last folder was some mild cause for consternation, primarily because the case belonged to Raider. Wagner was unable to close the file as the big man from Arkansas was still somewhere on the plains searching for Johnson Selks on behalf of the Helena sheriff. As far as the agency knew, Raider was still on the trail.

Wagner leaned back in his chair, removing his wire-rimmed spectacles, cleaning them with an ironed handkerchief. He always looked fit and dapper at his post, wanting to set a good example for the other men. Most of them followed his example, but there were a few exceptions. Raider never wore a suit, a tie, or a starched collar unless someone held a gun on him.

He put on his glasses and raised the file again for a meaningless look. It was routine. Nothing to worry about. Raider was always chasing someone like Selks and he always mastered his opponent.

Wagner dropped the file. Raider was his one loose end. He never gave progress reports during a case and he never asked for help unless he really needed it. A one-man troubleshooting crew. But for how long?

No one knew Raider's true age at the agency, not even Wagner. Raider was asked once and he replied that he was somewhere between thirty years of age and a meeting with the Devil. He claimed that everybody he had sent on ahead would be in hell to get even with him.

Raider's arrogance and humor used to irk Wagner before he finally got used to it. That was the big man's nature. You never really got to know him, you just got used to him.

Wagner looked at the name again. Johnson Selks. He tried to picture the man but came up with a blur. It was sure taking Raider a while to catch him. But then again, the hunted always had a quality of desperation that gave them stamina and quickness. Raider could summon up those qualities as well when he needed them. Wagner shuddered to think what damage the big man could have done had he turned to the wrong side of the law.

Wagner's head lifted when he heard the front door slam. He looked up to see one of the messenger boys employed by the agency. The lad was sweating and huffing for breath.

"Go back and close that door quietly," Wagner told the lad.

The boy ignored him, coming toward his desk. "Mr. Pinkerton is on his way down the sidewalk, sir. And he doesn't look too happy."

Before Wagner could scold the boy for his impertinence, the lad rushed toward the back room where the records were stored. Wagner had to smile. He could hardly blame the lad for fearing Allan Pinkerton's wrath. While Wagner had rarely been a direct target for his boss's ire, he had seen strong men laid to wreckage by a stern word from the big Scotsman.

"William, I'll see you in my office!" Pinkerton bellowed when he came through the front door.

Wagner just nodded and stood up from his desk.

The other clerks and agents held fast to their work, hoping the boss would ignore them.

Pinkerton took off his overcoat and hung it on a rack behind his desk. "Damned cold for June."

"Yes, sir."

"Ha!" Pinkerton sat down and folded his hands over his stomach. "Some days I don't know why I bother gettin' out of bed."

Wagner waited patiently, taking the chair opposite Pinkerton. He knew if he was silent long enough that his superior would vent the source of his anger. Pinkerton was not one for holding things in.

"That damned governor of Nebraska!"

Wagner raised an eyebrow. "I beg your pardon."

Pinkerton took out a telegram and handed it to his associate. "He's denouncin' the methods of one of our men."

Wagner read the angry response to a case he had closed that afternoon. The governor was not happy about the loss of two marshals who had been killed in a raid organized by Henry Stokes, one of their best agents. He intimated that Stokes had been careless.

"Ha!" Pinkerton exclaimed. "If you read Stokes's bloody report, you'll see clearly that the marshals were the ones bein' careless. Sure, two of them were killed, but that whole gang was captured in the bargain. They're gonna hang 'em all next week."

Wagner shrugged. "I wouldn't worry," he replied. "No official charges will be brought to bear against anyone. Even the governor knows that Stokes did what he had to do."

Pinkerton threw out his arms. "Then why did he write that nonsense?"

"Probably the chief marshal was upset at having lost two men," Wagner replied. "Things are not as rough down that way, at least not as bad as it used to be. The marshal is more used to serving papers than chasing outlaws. I wouldn't worry about it."

Pinkerton sighed, seeming to deflate somewhat. "Ah, I don't mean to be pratin' on like a schoolgirl. It just riles me when someone belittles a job well done."

That seemed to be the end of it.

Wagner started to excuse himself, but Pinkerton urged him to keep his seat. "Somethin' else came in over the wire," Pinkerton said.

Wagner read the lengthy message which delineated some sort of trouble in the cattle country of Montana. "So bad they're requesting a team of our men," Wagner said out loud. "I wish they'd gone into more detail."

Pinkerton grunted, leaning back, looking out the window. "Damned cold for June."

"I don't know how many men we can put in the field," Wagner offered. "I know Stokes is available, but who else?"

Pinkerton rose and looked at the huge map of the western

territories that covered a whole wall. "Who's out that way now?"

Wagner swallowed, his throat going dry all of a sudden. "I'm not sure."

Pinkerton looked over his shoulder, grinning. "Now, William. You can't trick an old trickster. Raider's in Helena, isn't he?"

Wagner nodded, but then added: "He *was* in Helena. He could be anywhere now. He's trailing someone and he could be forever finding him."

Pinkerton eased back to his desk, sliding into his chair. "Nevertheless, if we can get word to him, he can start the investigation immediately."

Wagner did not want to disagree too vehemently, as he could see that Pinkerton had already decided the matter. His only response was, "It could take a while before he's found."

Pinkerton grinned. "Then tell the bloody marhsal's office that he's theirs as soon as they can find him. We can put another man on the trail he's chasin'. This trouble sounds like somethin' for Raider."

"I'll get right on it, sir."

Wagner rose quickly and hurried back to his desk. He had a bad feeling about sending Raider in by himself. The marshal had requested a team of men. Of course, they could always send reinforcements later, but that might not save Raider's life.

Raider paid a price for being good with a gun. If there was a thick mess to deal with, Pinkerton always chose his surest shot for the task. Wagner kept waiting for the inevitable day when the telegram arrived to announce the death of the big man from Arkansas. Until then, he could only send him into the middle of another difficult investigation.

CHAPTER THREE

Raider felt a hand on his shoulder. He shrugged and threw his arm out, flailing at an imaginary assailant. The skinny man with the corncob pipe jumped back to avoid the open-handed strike. Raider sat up in the half-darkness to get his bearings. It took a moment to remember where he was and who he was after.

"Like wakin' a rattlesnake," said the skinny man.

Raider glared sleepily at him. "How long I been out?"

The man shrugged. "Hour, plus half again. Like you said. Just doin' what you asked."

Raider grunted, but it was hardly a sound of approval.

Corncob turned away, a bit peeved. "Can't fault a man for doin' what he's asked."

Raider nodded absently. "I reckon not."

He felt for his guns, next to the pallet on the floor. They weren't there. Raider leapt to his feet, grabbing the shirt of the skinny man.

"Where's my iron?"

The man showed no fear. "Big 'un, whynchoo just come on downstairs with me and see what I done for you. Then maybe you won't be so all-fired ready to think I'm like that boy you're chasin'."

Raider stomped down behind his host, keeping his hands ready for a fight. But there wasn't anything to fear under the roof of the corncob man. In fact, he surprised the hell out of Raider.

"There you go," he said softly. "Had ever'body goin' to it while you was out. Didn't have much time."

Raider's face went slack and his black eyes were glassy. Spread out on the wooden table in the center of the room were

14

his weapons, cleaned and oiled to a dull shine. He picked up his Winchester '76 and rattled the smooth lever. His Colt was next, spinning the cylinder and clicking the hammer.

"I musta been dead for you to get them guns away from me," Raider said, staring down the barrel of his .45.

The corncob man pointed the stem of the pipe at the Colt. "Peacemaker had a bit o' rust on it."

Raider nodded. "That it did, sir." He holstered the pistol.

The man clapped his hands. His wife came out carrying a large bowl of stew and a hunk of bread. Raider sat down and tried to eat slowly, but he was hungry enough to gulp his meal in less than two minutes. The woman put a wooden cup in front of him when he had finished chewing.

Raider looked up at her. "What's this?"

She glanced toward her husband.

Corncob replied: "Injun brew. Don't have t' drink it if you don't want."

The big man was still skeptical. "What's it do t' you?"

Corncob shrugged. "Some say it fights off the croup. Others claim it helps loosen the bowels. Might help you in that cold out there."

Raider drank it down in one gulp and ran immediately through the rain to the outhouse. When he came back out, he intended to give *what-for* to the corncob man but then decided that he felt better than he had in several days. His body was rested, his head clear.

As he strode back through the heavy downpour, he saw that the door of the house was open. The corncob man was on the threshold, just starting down the steps when he saw Raider coming. He led the big man to a tarp around back. A strong bay mare snorted under the canvas roof.

Raider's saddle was in place, along with his saddlebags. The woman came with his Winchester, sliding it into the scabbard on the sling ring. Raider checked the redwood handle of his low-slung Colt, just to make sure he had everything he needed.

"East is that way," said the corncob man. "Good luck."

Raider squinted at his gracious host. "Listen, back there when I was wakin' up. I didn't mean to be a bear."

"I think I'd druther wake up a grizzly," the man said with a straight face.

Raider felt ashamed and humbled. The man had done such a great job, getting him a mount in the middle of the night, oiling his guns, giving him food and a place to sleep. Now he was pointing the way in the darkness and the storm. There *were* good people on the plains, Raider thought.

He held out his hand. "Pleased to have knowed you, sir."

When Corncob clasped hands, Raider felt something cool pressing against his palm. He opened his hand to look at the double eagle. He gaped at Corncob who was smiling now.

"What's this about?" the big man asked.

"Don't like to overcharge a man," Corncob replied. "It ain't the Christian way."

Raider grimaced. "You sure 'bout this?"

"Just catch that thievin' scum and put 'im t' rest," Corncob replied. "Don't need his kind on the plain."

The woman handed Raider his shearling coat.

He did not take it. "After all you done, I hate to ask you . . ."

"Slicker's in your saddle bag," Corncob said matter-of-factly.

Raider felt himself blushing. "Even trade for the coat?"

"Done."

He pulled out the slicker and slipped it on. "Good fit."

"Godspeed to you, captain."

Raider looked back at the man. "What's your name, sir?"

Again, Corncob grinned. "Pardner, if I tell you, you'll forgit it afore you ride one danged mile."

The big man nodded. He led the mare out into the rain. She held steady, not spooking at all, even when it thundered. Raider swung into the saddle and rode hard to the east, never even looking back once to see the fading lights of the planked house.

Johnson Selks wasn't a hard man to trace. He had completely lost all sense of decency, robbing at his leisure whoever he came across. There was a stage outpost, a couple of sodbusters, and a Swedish family with a daughter that made eyes at Raider. Selks had robbed all of them, but he had not hurt anyone, not even the women. Maybe he just had one killing in him.

Raider figured he was close to catching up with Selks. The Swedes had seen him that morning, a good week's ride out of Rapid City. Heading for the Missouri River, the big man figured, and after that to Sioux Falls or maybe south. He rode away from the Swedes and the big blue eyes of the sweet daughter. He felt good to have sworn off women, that his abstinence would somehow help the cause. At least that was what he told himself.

The nasty weather broke before he reached the Missouri. A merciless sun beat down on the plains, baking everything dry in a couple of hours. Summer had finally arrived in one sweltering burst. The mare seemed to feel it worse than he did, so he had to slow. It did not matter. Johnson Selks would have to slow down too.

On the banks of the Missouri, he watered the mare and waited for the boatman, who was on the other side. After an hour or so, the ferryboat came toward him, easing along the line toward the shore. The boatman was a fat, ruddy man with hair sprouting from every pore in his body. His round face bore a look of hatred and regret.

"Damned scalawag!" he muttered.

Raider grimaced at him. "You okay, pardner?"

The boatman threw up his fat, hairy hands, raising them to Heaven. "Go ahead an' rob me, boy. Just pull your six gun an' let me tell you I ain't got nothin' more t' take. That other bastard cleaned me out."

Raider stiffened. "Selks!"

"He your pardner?"

"I'm chasin' 'im," Raider replied. "Grey hair on his head, smiles at you real nice and then . . ."

"Pulled iron an' told me t' give it all up," the boatman replied. "Waited till we was all the way across the river."

Raider led the mare onto the ferry barge. "Take me across quick and I'll see if I can get some o' your money back."

The boatman didn't have to be told twice. He started back across the Missouri with his lone passenger. His hopes had been spurred some and he went at his task with newfound enthusiasm.

"How long you been chasin' 'im?" the boatman asked.

Raider sighed, keeping his eyes trained on the opposite shoreline. "Since Helena, Montana."

The boatman chortled derisively. "Most men woulda quit."

"Most men woulda."

The boatman went on to say that he thought Selks was heading for Sioux Falls. Some said a stage route was now operating out of there, heading back east to the railroads. The east didn't seem as far away as it once did. Civilization was getting a chance in the west. Pretty soon Sioux Falls would be a real honest-to-God city and South Dakota would even be a state.

"Course, my day will end soon enough," the boatman went on. "When them stage coaches get out this way, won't need nobody t' ferry 'em over."

Raider looked skeptical. "Yeah? Why's that?"

"They'll build bridges," the boatman replied. "Hell, I couldn't get a stage on this duck boat anyway."

Raider couldn't imagine he'd ever see the day when a bridge spanned the Missouri. The old man was just daydreaming. Or maybe losing his mind.

When they were at the other side, the boatman stepped in front of Raider, blocking his path, stopping his exit.

Raider reached into his vest pocket for a silver dollar. "Don't worry. I'll pay you."

"Don't want your money," the boatman replied.

Raider looked puzzled. "Then what?"

"Somethin' I didn't tell that boy who robbed me."

"I'm listenin'."

"Crow country north o' here," the boatman offered.

Raider nodded. "I know. But them Injuns up there ain't been much trouble for a couplea years now."

The boatman shrugged. "Some say there's a young buck what left the reservation. Causin' some trouble hereabouts. Ain't killed nobody—yet. But there's been some strange stories comin' in off the plain."

Raider was losing time and patience. "Tell 'em quick."

"Well, this buck is the son of Growling Chief."

Raider frowned. "I heard Growling Chief died."

The boatman nodded. "Did at that. And the Crow nation

ain't been able to control that buck son o' his. Say the boy has
been stoppin' travelers an' forcin 'em t' trade with him. Only,
he gives 'em worthless things for their valuables. His braves
back him up with rifles."

"This buck got a name?"

"Well, some say he's called Killing Wolf, but others call
him Wolfbrand."

"Two names t' be reckoned with, I'd say." Raider pushed
past him, leading the mare onto the landing, swinging into the
saddle. "But whatever they call 'im, he can stop a bullet, can't
he?"

The boatman grinned from ear to ear. "Whoopee, lawman.
Go git 'im."

"I'm a Pinkerton," Raider replied from the back of his
mount. "And if you don't hear from me again, you'll know
that I can stop a bullet myself!"

With that said, he headed the mare east and rode hard away
from the river.

The trail was easy to follow. Selks had probably been the
boatman's only other passenger that morning, since there was
only one set of hoofprints leading away from the river. Those
tracks were deep because the ground was still softened by the
rain. Selks had an hour lead on Raider, maybe a little more.
He probably didn't know anyone was on his tail. With the
mare under him, Raider figured to give Johnson a surprise or
two.

The ground rose and fell in low, rolling mounds covered
with hundreds of summer flowers. If he had been on a picnic
with one of his favorite whores, Raider might have passed one
or two words about the beauty of the plain; but as it stood he
kept his eyes trained on the horizon.

As he rode on, the boatman's warning about the Crow Indians penetrated his consciousness. How seriously should he
take the boatman? Wolfbrand and his boys might have to face
a barking Winchester if they tried to impede Raider's chase.
Holding a rifle on an ignorant sodbuster wasn't very dangerous at all. An armed Pinkerton would offer more than a little
resistance.

Of course, they could always ambush him and kill him outright.

Why the hell was this Wolfbrand on the loose anyway? The Crow had settled down, those who hadn't fled to Canada. Did this young buck just have the Devil in him?

Raider slowed to let the mare catch her breath. He kept his eyes on the ground, watching the trail. It was too easy. Maybe Johnson Selks knew Raider was trailing him and he was laying a trap, waiting with a rifle behind a bush.

His black eyes scanned the horizon. Where was there to hide on the plain? He would be able to see anyone ahead of him, but then the same held true for the other. If a rider looked back, he might see the speck of Raider's mount as he approached.

He got down and walked a little and then got back on the mare. She was ready to run again, although he decided to pace her in the hot part of the day. No need to barrel headlong into an ambush.

At noon, it was so hot that Raider had to climb down out of the saddle and sit in the shade of his horse for an hour. He walked after that, until it was cool enough to resume the hard riding.

The ground was rolling higher and a few trees were growing at the crest of the ridges. Raider rode slowly through a shallow depression, listening to the sounds of song birds above him in the trees. He heard trickling water ahead of him and then the uneven splashing of something big.

He reined back and eased to the ground.

Shouting followed the splashing. It was one man, raving like a lunatic. He was hollering to the heavens, belching obscenities that would have made a buffalo skinner blush. Raider reached for his Winchester, cocking it quietly.

The shouting continued as he stepped softly through the depression, emerging to a sorry sight if he had ever seen one.

Kneeling in a muddy stream, his eyes turned toward the sky, was Johnson Selks. Beside him rested a dead horse, a scrawny black. That was just like his kind, Raider thought. Ride his mount into the grave and then blame the Good Lord.

Raider let go of a round that thudded into the water next to Selks. The grey-haired outlaw startled and fell backward into the stream. Raider levered the Winchester and aimed straight for Selk's head as he sat up again.

"You!" the outlaw cried.

Raider kept his eye on the sight. "Selks, if you give me any call, I'm gonna open up your brains and spill 'em in this runoff creek."

Selks started to move his hands. Raider fired the rifle. Selks grabbed the side of his head. A small trickle of blood ran down to his wrist.

"Damn you, Pinkerton! You shot off my earlobe!"

Raider found that he was smiling a little. "The next one is right between your eyes, boy."

Selks started to whimper. "Doggone it, you shot me!"

Raider felt sort of sorry for the old outlaw. He wasn't really much when you got up close. Just a wrinkled buzzard who had lived too long. Hell, back in his youth, he and Selks might have been friends. Things were different then.

"Come on, Johnson," Raider said, making him stand up. "Don't be bawling' on me. Hell, that trick back in Blackfoot Bend. Hell, that wasn't bad."

Selks glared at him and whined, "Yeah?"

Raider started to frisk him, finding several knives and a derringer. When he had tied Selks's hands, he led him out of the muddy creek so he could get dry. Selks became quiet for a while, sinking into his despair with the temper of a man resigned to his capture.

The big man from Arkansas had other things to worry about. They only had one horse between them. Then again, there wasn't any reason to rush. He could walk some and make Selks walk as well. It might take them a month to get back, unless they could pick up another mount along the way. Maybe in Rapid City. He grinned at the thought of the corncob man.

Raider wheeled back to Selks. "Johnson, where'd you hide that money you took from all them people?"

"In my saddlebags." He gaped mournfully at Raider. "I don't wanna go to the territorial prison, Pinkerton. I'm too old. I'll die in there!"

Raider went over to the dead horse. Water was rushing all around the animal. As Raider bent over, his face slacked and his gut churned. He looked up, holding the rifle in front of him.

Selks gawked as Raider splashed out of the creek and ran straight for him. "What is it, Pinkerton?"

Raider lifted him to his feet. "Your horse was killed by a Crow arrow, Johnson. You want t' hang round and see if they have an arrow for you?"

Selks stumbled forward as fast as he could.

Raider turned to follow, and then he saw them. They had been so quiet that he never even knew they were in the trees along the ridge. Now they were standing above him, about a dozen Crow braves with guns. And there was no way for him and Selks to get away from them.

CHAPTER FOUR

"Killin' Wolf," Raider said, lowering his rifle to the ground. "Or is it Wolfbrand?" He raised his hands to the sky.

The Indian dropped down in front of him, sailing off the rise above like he could fly.

"Dang it all," said Johnson Selks. "First I gotta get nabbed by a Pink, and now this long-haired buck is gonna kill me."

Killing Wolf moved toward Raider, coming face to face with him. The Indian's eyes were dull, almost colorless. Sallow, yellowish face, bags under his eyes, liquor smell on his breath. Killing Wolf had once been a proud, strong brave, but now he lived pretty close to a bottle. He was robbing to get whiskey money.

"Wolfbrand," Raider said again, peering straight at the intruder. "Kinda makin' a name for yourself in these parts ain't you?"

Killing Wolf did not say a word. He just reached for Raider's Colt, lifting it from the holster by the redwood handle. After examining the Peacemaker, he smiled at Raider and said, "Nice gun." Then he turned to regard Selks.

"Damn your red hide," the outlaw whined, "don't kill me, boy. Please. I'm a marshal and this one here done caught me and took my badge."

Killing Wolf thumbed back the hammer of the Peacemaker and put the bore against Selks's forehead.

His men, who were now gathering behind him, thought the sight was terribly funny. They laughed and passed a whiskey bottle between them. Raider felt a talon ripping across his gut, from the inside. All he needed was a bunch of liquored up renegades to slow him down. He was pretty sure they

23

wouldn't kill him, but they seemed to be set on making trouble.

Killing Wolf pulled the trigger of the gun, but not before he lifted it away from Selks's head. The loud burst no doubt deafened the same ear that Raider had shot the lobe from. Selks fell backward, crying and squirming on the ground.

Raider sighed, feeling sorry for poor Selks who didn't seem like much at all now that things weren't going his way.

Killing Wolf shot a glance back at Raider. "This man is no marshal."

The big man nodded. "No, he ain't that."

"He's a thief," the Indian replied.

"Some say the same 'bout a man called Wolfbrand."

Killing Wolf smiled. "That is not me."

"No, I reckon not."

The Indian pointed back at the pitiful figure of Johnson Selks. "That man is a thief. I know. My sister was traveling to Cheyenne, to bring back my brother who had been riding as a scout with the army."

"Your sister went by herself?"

"No," Killing Wolf replied. "She went with our brother's wife. My brother was hurt and his wife wanted to see him. The army said it was fine. But this man," he turned back to Selks, "robbed a stage stop and my sister was there."

Raider squinted at the renegade. "How you know 'bout that?"

His adversary smiled. "Can't you guess?"

Raider knew word had a way of getting around fast, even on a seemingly deserted plain. Maybe Killing Wolf had heard it from the boatman. It didn't really matter now.

"I'll take 'im back t' justice, Killin' Wolf," the big man offered. "He'll hang for what he done."

"I didn't mean to kill that man!" Selks cried suddenly, sitting up. "It was an accident. My gun went off by mistake."

"Four times?" Raider said.

Killing Wolf laughed. "Probably shot him in the back."

"All four bullets," Raider replied.

Killing Wolf handed Raider the Colt. "Pick up your rifle and go, black eyes. I will not make you stay here."

Raider gestured toward the fallen horse. "What say we have a look in them saddlebags afore I go?"

"Don't leave me with these savages!" Selks cried.

Killing Wolf's eyes narrowed. "You wouldn't try to save him, would you?"

Raider felt something give, like the plan he had cogitated would work—maybe. "Hell no, I don't care nothin' 'bout draggin' his worthless carcass all the way back to Montana. I just want to see what he stole."

Somehow this logic appealed to Killing Wolf, who sent one of his men to retrieve the saddlebags from Selks's dead mount.

They went through the plunder, identifying the things that belonged to Killing Wolf's sister and his sister-in-law. There was also plenty of money that Selks had taken along the way. Raider offered to take the money back to those who had lost it. But Killing Wolf had other ideas.

"When we hang him," the Indian said, "we will put the money in his pockets so he can buy his way into the spirit world of the white man's God."

Selks let out a bellyaching yowl. "Don't let 'em hang me, Pinkerton. I don't want t' die with no heathens."

Raider knew he had things under control, but he had to shut Selks up before he ruined the whole thing. He walked over and kicked him on the chin to put him out cold. This seemed to please Killing Wolf, who grinned broadly. His men also laughed aloud.

The big man turned back to Killing Wolf. "Hangin', huh?"

"You can't stop it."

"Didn't say I wanted to, Killin' Wolf. Hell, I'd like t' stick round t' see ol' Selks there get his just reward. I mean, if I took him back t' Montana, they'd lynch 'im for sure. So the way I see it, you're savin' ever'body a lot o' trouble by stringin' 'im up now."

Killing Wolf nodded curiously. "You make a lot of sense for a white man."

Raider started for his horse. "Say—I got a thick rope that'll do fine for a lynchin'. You boys know how t' make a noose?"

None of them did. Raider found the rope and went through a painstaking demonstration, winding each of the thirteen loops to make the unlucky knot. By the time he had finished, Selks was awake again, screaming his fool head off.

"I'll be glad when he's dead," Killing Wolf remarked. "He won't make nearly as much noise."

Raider forced a puzzled expression on his countenance. "Now where the hell we gonna hang this boy?"

"Please," Selks bellowed. "Don't kill me. I don't wanna die."

Raider wanted to tell him to play along, that things would work out fine if he just kept his mouth shut. But Killing Wolf and his men were on top of them, making Raider wonder if he would be able to pull off the trick. He had seen it once before, in Yuma. Doc had come up with it to get them out of a much worse jam. Now that the Doc had retired, the trick was Raider's.

"There," Killing Wolf said, pointing to the trees on the rise. "One of those is high enough."

Raider insisted that they hang Selks right then, but Killing Wolf and his boys wanted to drink some more. They all headed for the ridge, drawing from the bottle. Even Raider was offered a slug of the rotgut, which he took, to be polite. Inside, however, he was wondering how he could make the plan work.

On the hill, the Indians continued to drink. A couple of them left for a while, only to return with a dozen cleaned birds of some sort. They built a fire and roasted the birds for supper. Raider had to admit that the meat tasted better than chicken.

By the time evening rolled around, Killing Wolf and his men were stewed enough for Raider to try his move. He insisted that he should be the one to string Selks up, since he had chased him through two territories. Killing Wolf, who, in his stupor, was losing interest, agreed without a hitch.

It was then that Raider did it. Selks asked him what was going on, but the big man just told him to shut up. He managed to do it right in front of the Indians, who never suspected a thing.

When he had finished, he leaned close to Selks's ear. "You ever seen a hangin' afore?"

"I damn sure have. An' I don't want t'. . ."

"Shut up! An' stand still!"

Selks groaned as the big man from Arkansas slipped the noose around his prisoner's neck. Raider had to smile. It was perfect. All he had to do was get the hanging underway.

"On the horse, Selks!"

Killing Wolf let out a savage whoop.

Selks got to his feet, stumbling like a town drunkard.

Raider held his shoulder, whispering from the side of his mouth. "You said you seen a hangin'?"

"Yep, I . . ."

"Just nod."

Selks nodded as he walked toward the horse.

"You remember how the hanged men looked?"

"Yeah, I damn . . ."

Raider punched him lightly in the back.

Selks nodded.

"You better look just like one o' them hanged men when that horse goes out from under you."

Selks tried to stop and glare at Raider, but the big man pushed him toward the Indian pony.

Two of Killing Wolf's braves lifted Selks onto the back of the pony.

Raider tossed the rope over the branch of the tree.

Killing Wolf stepped up next to the horse as Raider tied off the rope. "You want to say any words to your God?" he asked Selks.

The outlaw shook his head.

Raider nodded at the renegade. "I figured I'd give you the honor o' slappin' that horse's behind."

Selks cried out for mercy.

Killing Wolf laughed and gave the horse's rump a stiff whack.

Selk's eyes bulged, his tongue lolled out. He strangled and then went limp. When he was motionless, one of Killing Wolf's men stepped forward and removed all of the stolen money from Selks's pockets.

"Thought you was gonna leave it on 'im," Raider said.

Killing Wolf laughed. "I guess he won't need it now."

One of the braves brought Raider his horse.

"You had better leave," Killing Wolf said.

Raider swung into the saddle, figuring it was good advice.

He looked down at the Indian leader. "If you run into Wolf-brand, tell 'im that he can't keep makin' trouble. Tell 'im that he had better get back t' the reservation before they send someone after 'im."

"Good-bye, white man."

Raider eased the mare down the incline and then spurred hard to the north. When he was out of earshot, he stopped the mare and climbed down. He could see the fire burning for a long time. But there was nothing he could do until the fire died and the Crow braves moved on.

In the first glow of a deep lavender dawn, Raider tiptoed toward the dangling man. He used the butt of the rifle to tap the feet that twisted in the morning breeze. Selks did not move. Maybe the trick had not worked after all. Raider nudged him a little harder.

"Selks. It's me, Raider. Open your eyes."

The outlaw's body stiffened to life. He coughed and choked for a second, but managed to say something. Raider cut the rope, dropping the outlaw with a rude thud.

Raider guffawed. "Reckon it worked after all."

As Selks gasped for more air, Raider lifted the noose off his neck. Then he severed the loose end that had been attached to the makeshift rope harness around Selks's torso. Doc had come up with the idea. Tie the noose so there was a long piece coming back down out of the knot. Put a couple of loops around the man's waist and chest and tie them together in back with a short piece tied to the belt of the man's trousers for safe measure. With the loose end tied to the harness inside the man's clothes, it looked like Selks had been hanging by the neck, when he was really hanging by his torso.

"Dang it all," Selks said, "I feel like my armpits is cut clean through."

"Better thank the Lord it ain't your fool neck."

Raider tossed the harness aside and then curled up the rest of the rope.

"Gonna untie my hands?" Selks asked.

Raider laughed. "Don't start in with me, Selks. Otherwise I'll find Killin' Wolf an' tell 'im the Great Spirit sent you back t' be hanged again."

But Selks had vain hopes. "You didn't save me from them redskins just t' take me back t' Helena t' hang, did you?"

"Sounds kinda stupid, don't it?"

Selks started to wail. "I aint' got no luck at all. Why didn't you just let 'em kill me and get it over with?"

Raider lifted Selks to his feet." 'Cause ever'bodys always gettin' mad when I bring back bodies 'stead o' prisoners."

"Damn, they're gonna string me up!"

Raider shrugged, guiding him toward the mare. "Maybe so. But you're gonna get a trial first. And it'll be almost fair."

Selks tried to smile. "Think so? Hey, maybe I won't hang. I killed that boy in self-defense. I really did."

"Back-shootin' ain't exactly self-defense, Johnson."

"They're gonna hang me for sure!"

Raider was tired of listening to it, so he told Selks to shut up before he gagged him with a bandanna.

Selks did his best, but he was naturally one to bemoan a downturn in his fortunes, so Raider ended up gagging him after all.

They headed west again, for the river.

Later that afternoon, Raider heard shooting in the distance. He levered the Winchester and kept walking toward the sound of the commotion. Selks heard it too and snapped to attention on the back of the mare.

Rifles, Raider thought. A lot of them. They rang up in loud echoes that died as quickly as they had come.

Raider jumped onto the mare and rode double until he could see the men ahead of them on the plain. The rifles had stopped for good, or at least it seemed that way. He rode slowly forward until he saw the blue uniform of a United States Cavalry officer.

The young lieutenant, along with several men not in uniform, worked at stacking bodies next to a large covered wagon. He flinched when he saw Raider approaching the wagon. The big man raised a hand to indicate that he was friendly. The lieutenant waved back.

Raider guided the mare closer and then got down.

"Would you care to identify yourself, sir?" the officer said.

"Pinkerton agent. Takin' this man back t' Montana."

The lieutenant just nodded and looked at the pile of bodies.

Raider took a quick glance himself, spotting a familiar face. "Killin' Wolf, eh? You boys tricked 'im, din't you? Dressed up like sodbusters till he came t' rob you."

"Very good," the young officer replied. "Yes indeed, had ten rifles waiting for him."

"I told 'im he was gonna get in trouble," Raider muttered.

The army man gave him a curious stare. "I beg your pardon?"

"I said, them kind never learn."

The officer stiffened. "No, they do not."

"One thing, sir."

"Yes?"

Raider sighed. "Well, it's a kinda small thing. You know that boatman on the Missouri, you know, west o' here?"

"I do know him."

"Well, I was wonderin' if you might take some o' his money back to him?"

The lieutenant nodded dutifully. "We shall do our best to see that all stolen property is returned."

Raider thanked him and asked the particulars of his outfit, particulars that meant nothing to him. He was just being cordial, hoping that the army man would sell him another horse. He was told he could take as many Indian ponies as he could catch.

Raider thanked him again and promptly caught three of Killing Wolf's strong horses. A fresh remuda would make the trip to Helena a lot faster. And with all the trouble that had transpired, there didn't seem to be much else that could happen along the way.

Until they started shooting at him in Montana.

CHAPTER FIVE

The summer heat broke a little when the cool winds swept down from Canada. It didn't get too cold and the rain stopped. With a big, clear sky and four good animals, the trip back through South Dakota went off without a hitch. Johnson Selks was somber, although at night when they camped, he tried to draw Raider into conversation. Even a desperado got lonely once in a while.

"Bet you was a rounder in your day, black eyes," Selks would say with his eyes transfixed on the fire.

Raider shrugged. "I had my wild times."

Selks eyed him with a restrained desperation. "Ever cross the law?"

"Spent a night or two in the *hoosegow* for fightin' drunk, but I never killed nor robbed, not without good reason anyway."

"You kilt plenty, I bet!"

Raider sighed and shook his head. "Maybe. But I never shot a defenseless man in the back."

Selks lowered his head and took his medicine. "I'm gonna ask God t' forgive me on the gallows."

"Ask now," Raider replied. "Y' never know."

They rode on, making northwest for the territory of Montana. Raider steered clear of Rapid City. He considered going back to see the man with the corncob pipe. The man deserved another word of thanks. But Raider did not want to take Selks into town as the outlaw might have kin or allies in the region and the best way to avoid people was to avoid towns.

Besides, Raider thought as they rode over the spreading bitterroot blossoms, Selks was working up to something. Raider could see it behind the hangdog expression. A quick glint, the eyes taking in the routine, a parting of the lips to reveal snarling brown teeth—it wasn't much, but it didn't fit with the repentant mood that was there the rest of the time.

Sure enough, the first night after they had crossed over into Montana, Selks gave it his best effort.

"Pinkerton, you ever commit any sins?"

Raider grimaced sideways at him, wondering where the strange question had come from. A signal flag went up inside the big man's head. Selks definitely had something in mind. But Raider figured to be ready.

"I asked you if you was a sinner," Selks insisted, his face contorted in the shadows of the fire.

"All men 're sinners," Raider replied.

Selks shook his head mournfully. "Lord knows I'm a sinner. And when I get up on that gallows, I'm gonna tell the whole world."

"Well, don't be s'prised if the world refuses t' care."

Selks laughed a self-deprecating chuckle. "Nobody cares 'bout me. I had a wife once but she died. Never gave me a child. You got any kin, Pinkerton?"

"Got a uncle back in Arkansas. I reckon he's still livin'."

"Any children?"

"None that I know of," Raider replied. "I ain't the kinda man to take a wife an' have a family. I'd get bored in a hurry."

"Cowboy, take these ropes off me," Selks said suddenly. "Let me sleep with my hands free. Look, my fingers is turnin' blue."

Without a word of protest, Raider got up and used his knife to sever the bonds of Johnson Selks. The aging outlaw looked up with a grim smile, like he figured to have the edge on this dumb Pink that would cut him loose. Raider turned to one side, his hand on his Peacemaker.

"Listen!"

Selks perked up, playing along. "What?"

Raider held out his hand. "Just stay put. Don't move."

With that, the big man from Arkansas strode out into the shadows where Selks could not see him.

When he was far enough away, Raider turned back and watched the outlaw. Selks did not waste any time untying the knots of the bonds on his ankles. As soon as he was free, he ran toward Raider's mare, leaping for the saddle. His foot hit the stirrup, but instead of bounding up onto the mare, the saddle slipped down and Selks thudded to the ground.

Raider laughed and strode back into camp. "April Fools," he said as he came into the orange circle of the firelight. "I loosened the cinch afore I untied you. Kinda funny ain't it?"

Selks wasn't laughing. He picked up the rifle that was slung on the saddle, rattling the lever. Raider looked into the bore of the weapon.

"I'm gonna shoot you with your own gun," Selks said.

Raider's hand fell toward his Colt.

Selks pulled the trigger, only to have the Winchester click harmlessly.

Raider grinned and thumbed back the hammer of the Peacemaker. "I took out the bullets when I loosened the cinch, Johnson. Drop it."

He made Selks tie his own feet and then Raider tied the outlaw's hands behind him.

"No more talk 'bout repentin' 'less you mean it," Raider said.

The sound of thunder caught the big man's attention. He turned his eyes upward to look at a clear sky. Not one cloud on the horizon. Still, the thunder persisted, not dying away like the rolling echo that followed a bolt of lightning.

"What is it?" Selks asked hesitantly.

Raider had to think before it hit him. "Cattle. And they're runnin' this way. A whole bunch of 'em."

Shots from rifles and pistols resounded in the darkness.

Raider kicked out the campfire and then dragged Selks to the safety of a knobby rise on the plain.

The cattle rushed around them, splitting the rise as they ran on to the southeast.

More gunshots. Slugs ripped into the dirt beside them. Raider had his Colt in hand but he could not see anyone to fire at. The cattle were gone suddenly, the last of the herd passing by as quickly as they had come. Voices hollered back and forth. More gunshots.

Raider huddled close to the ground, listening in the darkness. He could not guess the number of riders who were shouting and firing their weapons. A horse loped by him, coming within a few yards. Raider started to fire but he only caught a glimpse of the rider before he disappeared into the dusty night.

"He didn't see us," Raider whispered to Selks.

No reply from the outlaw.

"Selks."

He was lying motionless on the ground. Raider touched his forehead. Wet and sticky. Blood running down the bridge of his nose to his mouth. One of the stray rounds had caught him and ended his life.

The big man wondered if Selks had ever gotten around to really repenting his crimes.

But there were other things to worry about.

The horses had spooked during the cattle stampede. Raider tried to find them in the dark to no avail. He did manage to get back to his campsite, which had been thoroughly trampled. At least his saddle was intact. He used it for a pillow and stretched out for necessary sleep.

At first light, he saw two of the Indian ponies grazing not far from the camp. There was also a tall bay that Raider took to be the mare, but as he drew closer to catch the ponies, he saw that it was not his mare at all. The bay had a saddle and it was standing next to the body of a young man who had been shot in the chest.

"I guess me and Selks weren't the only ones with a run o' bad luck."

Raider caught the bay and then rounded up the Indian ponies. After he had loaded the two bodies on the ponies, he rode in a circle to search for other unfortunate souls who might have caught a slug, but there were no more. He studied the tracks and decided that four or five men on horseback had driven between thirty and fifty steers over the trail that night.

While he was examining the tracks, the bay mare wandered back, followed by the other Indian pony. Raider saddled her with his own saddle and decided to ride her instead of the dead man's horse. He considered moving the unknown corpse back onto the other bay—a man would want to ride his own mount, dead or alive—but decided that it was pointless.

He peered south, wondering if he should go after the cattlemen. They were probably rustlers, operating at night and killing people when they had to. But he had problems of his own. He turned northwest and rode on.

About midday, he saw the cloud of dust rising up in front of him on the horizon. Riders, probably close to twenty. The dust turned into tiny specks and then into armed men on horseback.

"What now?" the big man muttered to himself.

He was going to draw his rifle, but the men spread out and started to circle around him. He counted nineteen. Their rifle levers and pistol hammers all seemed to click at once.

When Raider did not make a threatening move, one of the men rode forward.

Raider tipped his hat, figuring to be polite to men who might shoot him—especially since he was outnumbered nineteen-to-one.

"How do, sir?" he offered with a coyote grin.

The rider did not answer, but rode around Raider and his lifeless crew. He sported a yellow mustache and the narrow-brimmed Stetson of a northern cowboy. Clear eyes that showed no emotion. Dressed like a rancher. He frowned at the bodies.

"Them is dead," he said to Raider.

The big man had to keep himself from laughing. "Got t' give you that one," he said casually. "Y' know a dead man when y' see one."

"I see two."

Raider glanced back comically. "Reckon y' do at that."

"That's Hardy Fillmore, and that bay's his horse," the rider said. "He's been gone two weeks, lookin' for somebody."

"He mighta found 'em," Raider replied. "I came on 'im this mornin'. He was shot last night by men drivin' cows to the southeast, or at least nearabouts as I can tell."

The rider perked up. "You saw 'em?"

"Heard 'em was more like it. Four or five riders, with say, forty head."

The man motioned for another rider to come out of the circle. When he was close enough, the first rider said, "This boy saw 'em."

"Maybe he's one of 'em," the second rider offered.

Raider squinted seriously at them. "I ain't."

"Then maybe you can tell us what you're doin' out here," the first rider said.

The big man gestured back to the corpse of Johnson Selks. "I was chasin' that boy for the sheriff in Helena. Had t' go all the way t' the Missouri River t' catch 'im."

The first rider looked at his companion and nodded. Then he glanced back at Raider and said, "Let Jimmy take these horses from you."

Raider shook his head. "Can't surrender custody o' Selks till I deliver 'im t' Helena. I'm . . ."

"We know who you are," said the man with the yellow mustache. "Jimmy, get those horses."

Raider wanted to draw down but he knew better with all the guns surrounding him.

Jimmy took the horses and started north with them.

Raider looked at the first rider. "What now? You gonna shoot me?"

The rider raised his hand.

This was it, Raider thought, the end of his career as a detective.

But the rider waved his hand and the others broke and rode south.

Raider glared at the man, who was now smiling.

"They won't find him," the man said.

"Find who?" Raider asked.

"Red Dog. Hardy was close, but look what happened to him."

Raider was trying to hold back his anger. "Just who the hell are you, mister?"

"I'm Junior Mays, deputy marshal for this section of the Montana territory. I been lookin' all over for you, Raider. You're a hard man to find."

"That's the truth. Mind tellin' me why you want me?"

Mays laughed. "Don't worry. You ain't in any trouble with the law. Not unless you count catchin' a thief an' a rustler to be trouble."

Mays turned his mount to the northeast. "Come on, there's a outpost not far from here."

Raider fell in beside him. "This all cleared with my boss?" he asked.

Mays nodded. "Yep. I got a paper somewhere that says so. I'll have to dig it out when we stop."

"I'll take your word for it. Ain't much on papers anyways." But there were other things to consider before he started a new assignment. "I got t' write a report an' tell the agency that I caught ol' Selks there."

Mays shrugged. "I wouldn't fret over that stuff. The sheriff'll send word to your boss. A man named Wagner said you was to work for us the minute we found you. If you're willin' to take the case."

That made sense to the big man from Arkansas. "This place we're goin'," he said to Mays, "has it got whiskey?"

Mays said it did.

"What say we settle all this over a couplea shots o' redeye?" Raider offered.

"Kinda early ain't it?"

"Nope. Not for me."

They spurred their mounts and drove hard to the northeast.

The store was a slapdash wooden structure near a place called Medicine Rocks. No one was there, but Junior Mays took the liberty of slipping in the window to find a bottle of whiskey and two glasses. They sat down in the shade of an old awning that served as a front porch roof. Mays poured them both a shot and they knocked it back.

"Don't usually take to drink this early in the day," Mays said. "Kinda hurt me to see old Hardy strung over a horse like that."

Raider took another shot and then asked what the man had been doing to run into trouble like he did.

Mays sighed. "He was lookin' for you, Raider. I sent him myself."

"He's a deputy?"

Mays shook his head sadly. "Nope, just a rascal. Not unlawful, but one of those kind who don't like to work much. He'd scout or ride with you. Even handled a gun pretty good."

The big man looked out toward the shimmering plain. "Not good enough."

Mays was quiet for a while, grieving in silence.

Raider figured the deputy liked the dead man, even if he was a slacker. "Them other boys that was ridin' with you. They deputies?"

Mays shook his head. "Nope. Just a posse I raised. They'll go down close to the border and then come back. I reckon I shoulda gone with 'em, but I needed to talk to you."

After pouring a third shot, Raider said, "I'm listenin'."

Mays stood up and used a stick to draw three lines on the ground. The lines converged at one point and spread out like the track of a three-toed bird. He drew a circle on one side of the lines and then pointed back to the place where the lines came together.

"Three rivers," he said. "Runnin' down from the north. Powder River on the east, Pumpkin River in the middle and the Tongue River on the West. They run south, makin' this land good cattle country. Plenty of water and good grass."

"I'm familiar with the terr'tory," Raider said. "What's the circle?"

"Forest," Mays replied. "Way west. But here's where the trouble is."

He drew a straight line across the three rivers. "Two spreads. Three Forks on the north. Owned by a man named Mac Wilson. South is the Delta Plain Cattle Company. Owned by one Asa Cantrell."

Raider nodded. "I follow you so far."

"Trouble with Three Forks," Mays continued. "Cattle been disappearin'. Rustlers. So quick, though, that nobody can catch 'em."

"How long they been operatin'?"

Mays took a deep breath. "Six months."

Raider frowned. "Nobody done caught 'em in half a year?"

"I'm shamed to say it. I can't come up with no excuses. I just can't catch 'em. They've took about three hundred head from the Three Forks ranch. So far we ain't brought in one man."

Raider leaned back in the shade. "Them that passed me was carryin' about fifty head. So they're hittin' once a month?"

Mays nodded dolefully. "Just when things settle down,

they hit again. Nobody's ready. And each time, we think it's gonna be the last."

"What about the Delta Plain Company? They been hit at all?"

May hesitated. "That's where it gets bad."

Raider chortled. "I knew there'd be a bad part. Let's have it."

"Asa Cantrell says he's been rustled too, but Wilson claims it ain't so. Says Cantrell's herd ain't lost a cow."

"Any way t' back that up?" Raider asked.

Mays shook his head. "Some men can count cattle pretty good, but there ain't no way t' tell how many steers Cantrell has. His spread is too big. Course, we'll have a better idea when the roundup is over. That's gonna be soon, too."

"I got a feelin' this gets worse."

Mays looked at him. "You're a smart one. Yeah, thing is, Wilson claims it's Cantrell and the Delta Plain boys that're stealin' his cows. Most of the sodbusters and settlers lean toward Wilson. He's got a good name in these parts. Come down from a family that's been here twenty-five years. Ain't never had no trouble with him."

"What about Cantrell?"

"Newcomer," Mays replied. "Only been here two years. He built a sizeable herd in that time. Wilson says Cantrell steals cattle all over the territory. But if he's rustlin', nobody's ever been able to catch him at it."

Raider stood up, stretching, mulling it over in his head. "You ever talk t' this Cantrell?"

"I have. He's ornery. Claims he just had luck with his prize bulls. Said he started his herd with cows he brought from Nebraska. I asked around but nobody could tell for sure. And I can't go all the way down to Nebraska to find out."

Raider sat down again. "Interestin', as my old partner used to say. Cantrell offer any explanation why his neighbor's cows is bein' rustled?"

"Red Dog."

"You sent that posse after 'im."

Mays nodded, exhaling. "They won't catch him, though. He just steals just enough cattle so he can move quick. And they won't chase him after he crosses the border."

"Mind tellin' me who this Red Dog is?"

"Some claim he's a half-breed Cheyenne Indian. Sometimes he has a dozen men with him. Sometimes half that. Did you get a look at any of them that was drivin' them cows south?"

Raider shook his head. "Not enough t' make a difference. Cheyenne, huh? Ain't been no trouble with 'em for a while."

"No trouble at all, 'ceptin' Red Dog. Most of them stay on the other side of the forests. Crow are up there, too, but farther north."

They sat quietly for a long time before Mays spoke again. "If all this ain't bad enough, Mac Wilson claims that Red Dog is workin' for Cantrell. Some even think Cantrell *is* Red Dog in disguise. But I ain't got any proof either way. And it just keeps gettin' worse."

Raider knew what that meant. "Range war."

"No militia up this way," May said defeatedly. "Ain't much I can do but let 'em fight it out. A range war could tear this territory apart, this end of it anyway."

"How come Wilson ain't already gone after Cantrell if he thinks he's so all-fired guilty?" Raider asked.

"Cantrell has at least ten hired guns workin' for him as well as his regular outfit. Wilson's tryin' to build a little army himself, but Cantrell has hired up most of the top shooters in these parts."

"Maybe he's usin' them gunhands as part of Red Dog's gang."

Mays slumped forward and put his face in his hands, rubbing his eyes. "It's too much for me, Raider. I'm the only law out this way. It's all I can do to keep up with the little bit of robbin' and killin' we got in these parts. The governor won't send me any more help."

"He sent me," Raider replied.

Mays laughed scoffingly. "One man. I'm one man, Raider. Even if we teamed up, I doubt we could handle all this."

"I work alone, Mays. No offense."

The deputy leaned back and looked at the tall Pinkerton. "You think you got a chance between these two outfits that's determined to kill each other?"

"I try not t' think on things like that," Raider replied. "I ain't one to face facts. Nothin' ever gets done if you face facts."

Mays threw up his hands. "Bein' as it lays, I wouldn't fault you none if you ducked out on this one."

Raider considered it. He could find a telegraph office and wire back to the home office that he wasn't going to take the case. But then what? They'd send somebody else and Raider's reputation would suffer when it got around that he had turned down a chicken pickin' job. He'd also have to think about it while he did train duty or something equally boring.

"Give me another shot o' that red-eye, Junior Mays, and then point me in the direction o' the Three Forks ranch."

Mays shook his head. "I reckon you Pinks is as crazy as you are good."

"Don't ever believe nothin' else, Junior. Now, how 'bout that hooch?"

As the deputy reached to pour Raider a shot, a rifle barked from the plain. Slugs slammed into the wall behind them. Raider dove for the ground, drawing his Peacemaker.

Mays just sat there in his chair, gazing out toward the direction of the shooting.

Raider stayed low, glaring at the deputy. "Are you crazy, boy? Somebody's shootin' at us!"

Mays squinted and then cried out: "Tinker, you crazy bastard, it's me, Junior Mays!"

No more shots.

Raider sat up, peering out over the plain. "You know who's shootin' at us?"

"He's just tryin' to scare us off," Mays replied. "It's Buster Tinker. He's the storekeeper here. Ain't around half the time. Here he comes now."

A round, balding man led a mule toward them. Two women sat on the back of the mule. They looked to be Indian or Mexican. Both wore new Calico dresses and had shiny black hair. They giggled when they saw Raider and Mays.

"Sorry to shoot at you, Junior," said Buster Tinker. "I seen two men and I didn't recognize your horse. What happened to that roan you was ridin'?"

"Sold it," Mays replied.

Tinker looked at Raider. "You gonna pay for that whiskey, mister?"

"He's the Pinkerton," Mays said quickly, fearing Raider's temper. "And he come to look into the trouble west of here."

Tinker nodded. "No charge then. Be glad to get rid of the trouble. Get things back to normal round here."

Raider relaxed some, though he was still uneasy about having been shot at. He tried to keep his eyes off the girls, who were pretty. He fought the urge to ask what Tinker was doing with two women on a mule.

Instead, he stuck to business. "Tinker, you know anythin' 'bout this mess?"

"Nothin' Junior ain't told you. Only thing is, if I had to side with one or the other, I'd say Cantrell is the snake. Don't trust him at all."

Before Tinker could elaborate, Mays intervened. "Tinker what the devil you doin' with these two squaws?"

Tinker snorted and looked scornfully at the women. "They caught me on the plain. Said they run away from the reservation. Said they want to live with me. Said they knew I had a store."

Mays glanced up at their bright faces. "That true, girls?"

They giggled and nodded.

"Git down off that mule," Tinker said hatefully.

"You gonna let 'em stay here?" Raider asked.

Tinker snarled at him. "What else can I do? I ain't got time to take 'em back to the reservation. Hell, that's two hundred miles from here. Junior, you want to take 'em?"

Mays shook his head. "Ain't my never mind. If I run into any Cheyenne or any army men, I'll tell them of your predicament."

Tinker made the Cheyenne girls climb off the mule. Then he turned to Mays and Raider. "How about y'all watch these two while I run up to Ekalaka?"

"Can't," Mays said. "Soon as I point Raider toward Three Forks, I'm on my way. I got to find that posse and see what they come up with."

Tinker turned to Raider. "Can I trust you to watch them and not run off with my whole store? I'll be back by tomorrow mornin'."

Raider looked at the two females. Evidently they knew he was being assigned to guard them, because they smiled and giggled at him. They sure were friendly.

He grinned at Mays. "Think I'll be safe with 'em?" he asked.

Mays shrugged. "I reckon, unless their bucks come after them. I wonder where they got them new dresses?"

Tinker turned the mule north. "Well, I'll be goin'. Y'all do what you like. I ain't one to sit while others bicker. Got business in Ekalaka."

The storekeeper started off on his errand. Both girls began to laugh at Raider. When he saw their eager faces, the big man from Arkansas decided to stay the night.

CHAPTER SIX

Junior Mays gave Raider directions to both the Three Forks ranch and the Delta Plain Cattle Company before he mounted and rode off to meet his posse. Raider walked his horse around to the back of the store, where a watering trough was full of fresh rainwater. The bay drank deep, as did the big man from Arkansas. He was considering a bath in the trough when he heard the giggling of the Cheyenne girls inside the house.

Their laughter reminded him of the pledge he had taken after Blackfoot Bend—to swear off women. Of course, that vow had been in relation to the capture of Johnson Selks, who was well on his way to the sheriff in Helena. Raider had also lost the necessary piety and smug self-satisfaction that came with swearing off anything, so all bets were off.

The back door opened and the two girls came out to shoo the horse away from the trough. Raider tied his mount to a ring at the corner of the structure and turned back to watch the Cheyenne ladies at work. They had cloth towels and a dipper, which led him to think they were going to wash some dishes inside the store. But to his wide-eyed amazement, the girls began to take off their dresses.

"What the hell?"

They just cackled with laughter.

The older girl regarded the big man for a moment, rolling her furtive brown eyes in a teasing leer. She then stepped into the trough followed by her younger sister. Raider thought he should not look, but he could not help himself. The girls began to soap each other, working up a generous lather.

Raider felt the old familiar disturbance that disconnected his thoughts. They continued to splash and giggle in the trough, either too immodest to care about his presence, or simply too savage.

"Y'all are dirtyin' that horsewater," Raider offered.

The older girl just gave him the same coquettish glance.

"I mean it," he insisted.

The young girl stood up, soap dripping from her brown nipples. "There's more water in the rain barrel around front," she said in a clear voice.

Raider couldn't argue with that.

The girl sat down and began to wash her big sister's back.

They weren't as large as Raider usually liked his women, but the smooth tones of their firm thighs presented possibilities.

Big sister was looking at him again, only this time she was not smiling. "Come in with us," she said softly.

Raider wasn't sure he had heard her correctly. "Maybe I better go round front till you're finished."

"Take a bath with us!" the girl cried in a louder voice.

Raider felt a rush through his body. He looked to both sides as if he were afraid that he was being watched. Both of them stared at him, awaiting his decision.

"Uh, I don't think that would be right," he said hesitantly.

But they had other ideas. They got out of the trough and practically stripped him bare. Raider did not protest. He figured if they pressed the issue that any responsibility on his part was ended.

The older girl gasped when she saw the size of Raider's erect member. Her younger sister was transfixed by the sight of the swelling organ. They grabbed him and pulled him into the trough.

The water was cold on his backside, but things warmed up when the girls took their places in front and in back of him.

At first, the horseplay was innocent. They did most of the groping, running their hands over his stomach. The older girl would not let her sister touch his prick, although she herself did not hesitate to take it into her hand. She had soft skin, nothing like a hard-working squaw.

Raider watched as she stroked him. "Where y'all from?" he asked.

She let go. The younger girl reached for him but her sister

knocked her hand away. Raider wondered if the older one wanted him to top her.

"My husband was a preacher," big sister said. "We was on our way to Fort Laramie when my sister and I ran away."

"You gonna go back to 'im?"

She gripped his cock again. "Not right now."

The younger girl whined at them. "You won't let me."

"Shut up," her sister replied. "You're too young."

"I want to kiss him," she insisted.

A doe-eyed look from the elder. "Will you give her a kiss? Maybe she'll shut up then."

Raider gave the girl a little peck. But she wanted more so they did it again. Then big sister wanted a kiss so he could do nothing more than oblige her. Pretty soon they were all kissing and rubbing against each other in the trough. Raider grabbed the older girl and tried to put his cock inside her.

"Not yet," she said, stepping out of the trough. "I want to do it on a bed. Tinker has a bed inside."

Raider stood up too. "All right, let's hurry." He was pretty worked up. The whole thing had happened before he really had time to think about it. Now he wanted the girl under him.

"I want to watch," little sister insisted.

Raider shook his head. "No siree, missy. I gotta draw the line somewheres. This is gettin' too strange."

The older girl pouted. "If you don't let her watch, I won't do it with you. Understand?"

Raider gawked at her. "Well maybe I'll just throw you down an' do it t' you right here on the spot. Without your say-so!"

She smirked at him. "You ain't that kind of man."

She had him pegged. Women always knew what was going on inside a man. Raider wasn't the kind to take something that wasn't offered freely. And he usually balked at a conditional offer.

"Damn," he muttered. "Maybe if I have a drink o' whiskey."

He gathered up all his gear and took it inside. The older girl wrestled his dirty clothes away from him so she could wash them in the trough. He was gulping his third shot of red-eye when she came back inside, holding her sister's hand.

"Well," she said smartly, "we washed your clothes. Now are you going to do what we say?"

Raider gestured with his hand. "Come here, punkin."

They hesitated, but then moved next to him.

Raider stroked their wet hair. "Y'all got names?"

"I'm Bright Feather. My sister is Little Bright Feather."

"Pretty names," he replied. "Little Bright Feather ain't never had a man before, has she?"

Bright Feather shook her head.

"How old 're you, Bright feather?"

"Nearly twenty!"

"And your sis?"

Her voice diminished some. "Fifteen."

Raider whistled. "God forgive me for bathin' with 'er. Tell 'er t' get on 'er clothes."

"What about me?"

"That's up to you," he replied. "You're a grown woman. I'm a grown man. You name it."

She touched his thigh. His cock sprang back to life. Raider looked into her dark eyes. She wanted it. He knew that much.

"Get on your clothes," Bright Feather said to her sister. "I'm going upstairs. You got a name, cowboy?"

"Raider."

"I'm going upstairs with Raider."

They went up to the second floor where the storekeeper had an old feather bed. Bright Feather climbed on the mattress and spread her dark thighs. Raider leaned his rifle on the wall next to the bed. Then he slipped down beside her and stroked her tight curves.

"You really are a beauty," he said to her. "I bet your husband misses you."

She scoffed at him. "He's a drunk. Preaches on Sunday, drunk on Monday. A real slob. I hate him."

Raider smiled. "Where'd you learn to talk so good?"

"My husband lived with a white family when he was younger. He taught me. He doesn't even speak Cheyenne."

"The boy can't be all bad."

"No more talk," she replied, trying to pull him down on top of her.

Raider took it slow. She was petite and he didn't want to

hurt her. After a long time of stroking and kissing, he entered her and filled her with his manhood. Neither one of them wanted it to be slow after that. They made a ruckus on the bed until Raider collapsed on top of her.

He rolled over and pulled her into his chest. "Thank you, honey. That helped a whole lot."

He heard giggling. Bright Feather wasn't laughing. She had closed her eyes for a nap.

"Dern you, girl!" he cried.

Little Bright Feather was peeking at him from around the door. She had crept upstairs and watched the whole thing. Raider got up to shut the door.

"Do it to me!" she insisted.

"I ain't one for poppin' cherries," he replied. "Now git on outa here."

She reached for his prick but he knocked her hand back.

"I want you to do it to me!"

He closed the door and propped a chair against it. "That sister o' yours is a pain in the saddle."

But Bright Feather did not hear him. She was snoring on the bed. He figured it took a lot of energy to run away from a husband. He wondered if anyone would be looking for her, and if it was wise to have someone else's wife in bed with him, but in spite of any second thoughts he found he was ready again. The fight with the little sister had excited him.

Raider reclined on the mattress, his body slumping together with Bright Feather's. "Hey, wake up. I got somethin' for you."

She came out of her nap as eager as she had been before. They coupled again and Bright Feather went right back to sleep. She was a strange one.

Raider lay beside her, suddenly wide awake. He looked up at the ceiling, considering what the marshal had told him. Two warring ranchers—nothing new on the plains. Accusations of rustling. A villain named Red Dog. This one sure as hell wasn't going to be boring.

He closed his eyes after he thought it all out. His slumber was dark and dreamless, only to be interrupted by the smell of food from below. He woke up in the last heat of the afternoon to find that Bright Feather was no longer beside him. He got up and found his clothes, dry and fresh on the chair.

When he was dressed, he went downstairs to find the girls cooking. Bright Feather did not even look at him, nor did her little sister who was still angry at Raider for not topping her. Without a kind word, they served him beans and cornbread prepared from Tinker's supplies. As he ate, the big man thought he should leave a couple of dollars for the storekeeper when he left.

He patted his full belly and visited the whiskey bottle again.

The girls cleaned up the dishes, as well as sweeping out the dust from the downstairs rooms.

"This place is dirty," Bright Feather said, coughing.

Raider nodded. "There's no shortage o' dust on the plain. How long y'all figure t' stay with Tinker? Till hubby comes lookin' for you?"

Bright Feather shrugged. "Who knows? We'll stay with Tinker till he runs us off, or till something better comes along."

Raider figured there was some sort of female logic behind a plan like that. "Well, if Tinker is one t' like women, then you'll have a home for a while."

Bright Feather turned suddenly to look sideways at him. She motioned upstairs, toward the bedroom. Raider winked at her.

Little Bright Feather caught on to their furtive communication. "You're going to do it again, aren't you?" she said dolefully.

Raider sighed and considered the offer. He was sated at the moment, ready more for resuming his nap than a tumble. Bright Feather seemed intent on having her way again.

"Let's hold off," he said. "I'm goin' t' take another drink outside. It's coolin' down some."

He went out with the whiskey bottle.

His eyes stared north as he drank. He was thinking he should get an early start in the morning. Both spreads were looking for hired hands, particularly those good with guns. Maybe he could pretend he was in search of work and infiltrate one of the outfits. But which one?

Suddenly, without any warning, Bright Feather whooped

and came running outside. She squinted to the north and shook her head.

Raider peered in the same direction. "What?"

"Riders," she said. "Five of them."

He did not contradict her, although he was skeptical until he saw the bumps moving on the plain.

"Git inside," he said.

"But . . ."

"Now!" he ushered her into the house and then found his guns.

"Who is it?" Little Bright Feather asked.

Raider started for the front door. "Nobody. Y'all just stay back. If it's your husband, you better be ready t' go with 'im."

He rushed out and stood in front of the store, crooking the rifle in his arm, waiting as the riders drew closer.

Bright Feather had been right when she said five riders were coming. He counted them when they were close enough. They saw him too, but just kept moving for the store. They looked worn, like men who had just made a hard ride.

Raider held the Winchester steady as they approached.

The lead rider stopped, prompting the others to rein up behind him. He was a large man, wearing rancher's clothes. Big bones, fair skin, an angular face. His lips were thin and peeling from the sun. He moved forward again but the others stayed put.

When he was close enough, Raider saw the steely circles of his blue eyes. "Where's Tinker?" he asked.

Raider nodded north. "Went up t' Ekalaka on business. Asked me t' mind th' store while he was gone. If you boys is lookin' for supplies, you'll have t' deal with me."

The man shook his head. "Just want to water."

Raider looked at the roan gelding the man was riding. "Your mount is lathered. You been runnin' hard?"

"What if I have?"

"Have t' water at th' rain barrel," Raider replied. "The trough is full o' soap."

The man nodded like he understood. He waved for the others to approach. His narrow-brimmed Stetson came off to reveal a thick head of red hair. As the riders came up, one of them called him Mr. Cantrell.

Raider's head jerked up. "You Asa Cantrell?"

The man nodded. "That I am. Do I owe you money?"

Raider lowered the barrel of the rifle from the crook in his arm. "No, sir. Not yet anyways. Maybe you will if I ask you for a job an' you see fit t' give me one."

Cantrell's steely eyes narrowed. "What kinda work you lookin' for?"

Raider smiled. "Let's say I'm not much of a cowpuncher."

"Then you ain't workin' for me," Cantrell replied.

"Not even as a gun hand?"

Cantrell's men stopped still in their tracks. Hands lowered to the butts of pistols and rifles in scabbards. Cantrell himself threw back the cloth of a thin duster to reveal an oiled sidearm.

Five against one. Not good odds, Raider thought. He still had the rifle. He stood there, waiting for someone to move.

Asa Cantrell leaned forward, his hands folded on his saddle horn. "You ain't got a chance against five guns, honcho."

Raider stood steady, forcing a coyote grin. "That may be so. I couldn't get all o' you. No I couldn't. The question is, how many would I get?"

Cantrell chortled. "Who told you I was lookin' for gun hands?"

Raider shrugged. "Some marshal named Mays."

"Mays would never send me any men," Cantrell offered. "He don't want none of this. He wants to go back to chasin' drunks and gamblers."

Raider gave him a stern look. "Didn't send me nowheres. He just up an' asked me if I was one o' them hired guns ridin' for Asa Cantrell. When I told him no, he suggested I get out o' this terr'tory in a hurry."

"Sounds like bullshit to me," a lone voice said from behind Cantrell.

Raider shifted his black eyes to the man. He was all hair and muscle. Low forehead that wrinkled over his nose. A fat head. Big hands that could pound a man dead into the ground without any coffin.

"Shut up, Lockett," Cantrell called over his shoulder.

Raider laughed. "Lockett? Ain't that somethin' a little lady wears round her neck?"

The man bristled, but a harsh word from Cantrell stopped him from getting down off his horse. Lockett pointed a fat finger at Raider. "You're mine."

Cantrell turned his horse to one side and glared at his hired hand. "That's enough out of you." Then to Raider, "You too."

The big Pinkerton nodded. "Ain't lookin' t' fight nobody. If y' don't want another tough hand, maybe I'll find somebody else round here who does. That marshal said you was butted up agin one o' the locals."

Cantrell reached into his pocket for a plug of tobacco. He bit off a chaw and worked up a good spit. "Ain't too popular with the marshal," he said as he spat a glob of brown juice at the ground near Raider's feet. "Nor nobody else for that matter."

"Looks like I ain't neither," the big man replied.

Cantrell eyed him coldly. "What else that marshal say?"

Raider decided to play it as truthful as he could. "Said he was chasin' some boy name a Red Dog, t' th' southeast. Said he took some cows from a spread called Tree Forks."

"*Three* Forks," Cantrell corrected testily. "And that just goes to show you how stupid a lawman he is."

Raider frowned. "Come again?"

"We was chasin' Red Dog ourselves," said the man named Lockett. "Had him runnin' dead north from here. Stole fifty of our steers last night."

Raider did not say a word. He considered that five men on horses had passed him in the southeast. Now here was Cantrell, a main suspect in the rustlings, showing up with four men on lathered horses. Maybe Cantrell had enough time to stash the cows and double back to ride down from the north. They seemed to be a sly, wary bunch.

"That marshall will never catch Red Dog," Cantrell offered.

Raider nodded. "He did seem a mite put off by the whole thing. I can tell you I wasn't too pleased when he told me t' light out o' here."

"You want a job, cowboy?" Cantrell asked all of a sudden.

"Ropin' or shootin'?" Raider replied.

Before Cantrell could reply, the man named Lockett let out with a raspy sound of derision. "Shit, that boy cain't do neither. He ain't tough enough t' ride with us."

Cantrell studied Raider's face. "Maybe he's a lawman. Lawmen don't like to fight. How do you feel about fightin', big man?"

"Name's Ray," Raider replied. "An' I can take that fat tub o' guts named Lockett on the best day he ever lived."

Lockett started to climb off the horse. "He's mine, Mr. Cantrell."

Cantrell spat a long, brown juicer. "You can have him, Lockett. If he gets by you, then I'll hire him."

Raider put down the rifle. He tried to remember how long it had been since he had a good fight. Lockett looked pretty slow, but he was mean and big. Raider reminded himself that he was big and mean as well.

Cantrell and his men dismounted and drew off to one side, standing in front of the store. As Raider and Lockett moved to face each other, the two girls came out of the house to watch the fracas. They had on their new dresses and immediately caught the eyes of Cantrell and his crew.

"Where'd they come from?" asked the red-haired boss. "I never knowed Tinker to have no squaws. Specially two girls as pretty as these."

The Feather sisters giggled and flirted.

Raider turned to tell the girls to get back inside the store, but Lockett chose that blind moment to rush him headlong and knock him to the ground.

Cantrell's boys started to root for their man.

Lockett was a fair country wrestler, pinning Raider with his superior weight. Raider grappled with him until he managed to get a hold on Lockett's neck. His fingers went white as he squeezed the muscles on both sides of the man's fat neck.

Lockett cried out and brought up his fists to hit Raider in the face.

Some of the fat man's weight shifted back. Raider heaved with his whole body, rolling Lockett aside. Raider jumped to his feet and planted a foot in Lockett's ribs.

"Hey, no kickin'," said one of Cantrell's men.

Raider backed off and put up his fists. "I'm ready either

way," he huffed, "You can back off any time, Lockett."

Lockett staggered to his feet, holding a hand to his ribs. "I'm gonna make you pay fer that kick."

"Looks like you're the one who's gonna draw his wages!"

Lockett rushed again, but this time Raider was looking at him. The big man side-stepped him, following the fat man's motion with a swift backhand to the rear of his skull. Lockett stumbled into his rooters, who had to catch him to keep him from falling to the ground.

They shoved him back at Raider, but not before one of them could say, "Maybe you oughtta think about givin' it up, Lockett."

There did not seem to be any quit in the man. He stalked Raider, grunting as he launched one awkward blow after another, hitting only the air as Raider's footwork kept him well out of range. Each time the fat man lunged at him, Raider ducked and threw a short left that stung the end of Lockett's nose.

"His face is bleeding," cried Bright Feather.

Her sister hid her eyes as the streaks of crimson flowed down Lockett's dirty countenance.

The fat man was reeling, so Raider decided to end it in a hurry. He lifted an uppercut that landed on the point of Lockett's chin. He grunted and went down to one knee.

Raider expected his opponent to give it up right then, but suddenly Lockett leaped toward him like a wolf springing off a fallen log.

As the maneuver caught him completely by surprise, Raider moved too late to avoid the charge. Again he tumbled backward and Lockett was on top of him with his wrestling moves. Raider felt the breath go out of him. Lockett pressed like a mountain of lard.

"The fat boy's got him now," Cantrell said. "Looks like I'm gonna have one less on the payroll."

The other boys whooped it up.

Raider freed a hand and brought his fist squarely against Lockett's ear. He felt a jolt through the thick ton of flesh. He hit the ear again. Lockett cried out like a wounded elk.

In a move his old partner had taught him, Raider spun out from under the fat man. He got up quickly, catching his breath, watching as Lockett stood up again. He couldn't have much left, Raider thought.

"Gonna kill you . . . gonna . . ."

Lockett stumbled toward him, trying to hit him with open paws.

Raider flung a roundhouse right that sent the tub of guts flying back on his buttocks.

Lockett grunted and then made a low groaning sound that was almost like a youngster crying.

Raider glanced at Cantrell, who was frowning. "Your boy is whipped, Cantrell. If he'll admit it, we can stop this thing right now."

"No!" Lockett cried.

Raider turned back to his adversary. Lockett was up now, still reeling but ready to take it to the end. In his hairy hand he held a huge buffalo skinner's knife. The blade looked to be a foot long.

"I'm gonna cut out your gizzard, black eyes."

Raider reached into his boot and brought out a hunting knife that was half the size of Lockett's buff-sticker. "I can't allow that," he said, grinning. "Let's see who wants t' die first, Lockett."

Lockett made one lunge, missing Raider's belly before the gun went off.

Both fighters were startled. They turned to see Cantrell holding a Colt that had been fired at the sky. He lowered the weapon, aiming at them, telling them to drop the knives.

Lockett frowned, his face a bloody mess. "But boss . . ."

"No need for you to kill each other. This man has fought you fair, except for the kickin', which he didn't know about. You rushed him blind, too, so that evens it."

Lockett thought twice, but then dropped the knife. Raider did the same. They stood toe to toe again.

"Come on, Lockett," said one of Cantrell's hands.

"Yeah," urged another. "Nobody at Delta Plain never whupped you."

The brief lull and the words of encouragement renewed Lockett's spirits. He was used to being the baddest bull in the pasture and he was not about to ruin his reputation if he could help it. He rushed one more time, trying to get Raider in a bear hug.

But he was too slow for the big Pinkerton. Raider backed up, popping him at will with the left until the blood flowed fresh on his face again. He finally threw a hard right to the gut that made Lockett buckle over.

The girls broke out in a sudden cheer for Raider.

He lifted an uppercut that sent Lockett tumbling in the opposite direction.

The fat man lay there for a while, groaning, trying to get up. But he was finished and when he finally managed to stand up, Cantrell would not let him fight anymore. He pushed Lockett toward the others and told them to clean him up. The squaws followed to help with his wounds.

As they led the beaten man to the rain barrel, Cantrell turned back to Raider. "I suspect you'd have to kill him before he'd stop."

Raider nodded, examining his raw knuckles. "I ain't seen many more who had his heart."

He looked up to see a strange glint in Cantrell's shiny eyes.

"Somethin' botherin' you, Cantrell?"

"Who are you?" asked the red-haired man.

"Ray Thornton." It was a name he used sometimes. Ray was close to Raider so he didn't have to worry about a mix-up, although it could be confusing when he was addressed by the surname. "I like t' be called Ray."

"Who said anybody figures to call you anything?"

Cantrell was square to him. Raider wondered if he was going to pull the Colt again. Raider didn't have a weapon. If Cantrell wanted him dead, why didn't he let Lockett try to kill him with the buff-knife?

"Say what's on your mind, Cantrell," Raider answered as he calculated the distance to the rifle leaning against the store.

Cantrell moved between him and the rifle. "Who are you to ride in here and whip a man who's whipped ever'body in this whole end of the territory?"

"I reckon I'm just tougher."

The red-haired man pointed a finger at him. "You're somebody. I mean *somebody*. You a big gun lookin' to make some money?"

Raider bent to ease the knife back into his boot. "Who I am don't make a diff'rence. If you don't want t' hire me . . ."

"Didn't say that!"

Raider came up with a derringer from the other side of his boot. "Then let me ride out o' here and I won't be botherin' you no more."

Cantrell eyed the derringer. "Who are you?"

"Like I told you—Ray Thornton."

"You're quick. Whoo-wee. I heard of a man named Birch, Henry Birch. Rode south of here, in Texas and Arkansas. Quick with a gun. Always carried a derringer and a knife in his boot."

Raider gestured toward the men who were tending Lockett's wounds. "You ask all these questions o' that bunch when they hired on?"

"They ain't as dangerous as you," Cantrell replied, keeping his eyes on the derringer.

Raider flipped the small weapon in his hand and tossed it to Cantrell.

The chief of the Delta Plain Cattle Company caught the derringer and examined the bore. "Thirty-two caliber?" he asked.

"Thirty-six," Raider replied. "You want t' give it back t' me?"

Cantrell hesitated but then gave the derringer up.

"If you don't want t' hire on no top gun hands, Cantrell, then I'm shovin' out o'here. There must be somebody'll hire me in these parts."

He started toward the store, showing his back to Cantrell.

"A dollar a day," offered the red-haired man.

Raider wheeled, regarding him skeptically. "Three dollars."

"If you ranch some."

Raider knew how to handle cows, although he had never liked cowboying very much. It might give him an opportunity to cover some territory during the roundup. It was too good to pass up.

"All right, Cantrell. but we got t' trust each other."

"You just turned your back on me," the rancher said. "Ain't that trust enough?"

Raider glared straight at his new boss. "If you'da gone for your gun, there'd be a bullet hole in your forehead."

Cantrell grimaced with a strange expression. "You're somebody big, all right. And whoever it is, it ain't Ray Thornton."

"I'll meet up with you in the mornin'. I got t' stay here t'night and watch these squaws for Tinker."

Cantrell shook his head. "Better come on with us. Tinker might not be back for days."

"Said he's comin' back t'morrow," Raider offered.

"What Tinker does and what Tinker says is two different things. Where the hell did he get them squaws anyway?"

Raider shrugged. "Said he found them wanderin' on the plain."

Cantrell tipped back his hat, staring toward the western horizon where the sun hung low, ready to dip back into night. "Their bucks might be comin' after them."

"I doubt it."

Cantrell looked at him. "Why you say that?"

"That oldest one said she married a preacher. Said he was a Cheyenne boy raised by white people and the Good Book."

The red-haired man sighed, showing more age in the shadows. "Dog me, just when I figured I'll never see nothin' new again, I find somethin' else."

Raider thought he saw the man's guard go down. "Just where do you hail from, Cantrell?"

Narrowing eyes from the boss of the Delta Plain. "I ask the questions, cowboy. You answer 'em and do what I say. Otherwise, you're back on the trail."

"You ask a lot for three dollars a day."

Cantrell strode quickly away, throwing over his shoulder: "If you don't want the work, move on."

"Cantrell!"

The shout made the red-haired man turn and draw his pistol. He was fast. Maybe as fast as Raider. Cantrell spun his Colt, a new Peacemaker, and dropped it back into his holster.

"No need to deny it," Cantrell said. "I suspect you and me are the top guns now in my outfit. But it's still my outfit. I wouldn't try to challenge that if I was you."

Raider had taken a chance with the trick, but it had paid

off. At least he knew where the real danger lay. As Cantrell strode back toward his men, Raider put a few things together. He decided Cantrell was the kind of man who could disguise himself as a rustler. And now Raider was working for him.

As it turned out, Raider did not have to stick by his promise to watch the Feather sisters for Tinker because they decided to go to live at the Delta Plain Cattle Company. The older girl had already announced her intention to marry Asa Cantrell before they left the store.

Raider thought this claim to be somewhat rambunctious, until he noticed that Cantrell and the others did not make light of it. He wanted to ask the girl if she was serious, but then decided that it did not matter. He had better keep his eyes open for other things that were more important—like proving the popular theory that Cantrell was really Red Dog, the rustling half-breed.

When Lockett's wounds were tended and the horses watered, Cantrell said they had better get moving while there was still light. Raider mounted up and moved along with the others. He hoped they would talk as they walked toward the purple horizon, but Cantrell and his men were tight-lipped. Raider figured their silence was due to the presence of the squaws. Hard men often did not like to talk around women of any kind.

"How far to the Delta Plain?" Raider asked.

Lockett looked back at him, not smiling or frowning. "Five miles," he said blankly. "It'll be near dark by the time we get there."

His defeated tone let Raider know that the fat man was not going to be any more trouble. Still, neither Lockett nor any of the other men elaborated on any subjects of interest or boredom. Raider held his tongue, not wanting to appear anxious. If Cantrell was Red Dog, sooner or later he would pull Raider into the action. An outlaw always needs his best guns in a fracas.

They rode on quietly until Cantrell raised his hand. Everyone stopped at his command. Raider eased up to see what he was looking at.

"Move aside," Cantrell said. "Let them pass."

They gave way to ten men on horseback who were escorting a surrey coach. As they passed, Raider caught sight of the driver and the woman beside him. The man with the reins in hand did not look familiar, but something about the woman made him sit up straight. It was hard to tell in the fading light, but the woman looked damned familiar.

He shook off the strange feeling that rushed over him. She couldn't have been anyone he had known before, at least not in Montana. She just resembled someone from his past. But who?

Cantrell came up beside him as the entourage rode past. "Wilson and his wife," he said bitterly. "Thinks he owns the whole goddamn territory. If I wasn't outgunned, I'd have it out right now."

Raider thought his new boss surely seemed to hate his rival. But did he hate him enough to steal from him? He'd find out soon enough, probably. Until then, he could only turn his bay mare and ride on for the Delta Plain with the others.

CHAPTER SEVEN

For some reason, Raider expected the Delta Plain spread to be a run-down shambles of a ranch. He supposed later, when he learned that the place was exactly the opposite of ratty, that he had based his prejudgment on the appearance of Cantrell and his four riders. They were dusty, ragged men who worked hard between baths, spending most of their time in the saddle.

Had they really been chasing Red Dog to the north? There was no way to be certain that Red Dog had been the one who passed Raider near the border, heading southeast. Maybe Red Dog was working both herds.

Raider shook off his thoughts as they loped into the Delta Plain Cattle Company. Cantrell raised his hand to several men who stood by a large corral to the left. Out beyond the corral, as far as Raider could see, stretched one holding pen after another—large circular corrals of barbed wire and pine posts. The first three pens were full of steers. Raider wondered if Cantrell really had enough cattle to fill the rest of them. He seemed to be expecting a huge roundup.

Cantrell reined up next to the men. He motioned the riders on, except for Raider. "Big 'un, you hold."

Raider eased the mare to a stop, keeping his eyes down, hiding them under the brim of his Stetson. He had a queasy feeling in his gut. He was suddenly afraid of being recognized as a Pinkerton agent. If Cantrell had hired anyone who had crossed his path before, there might be some guns drawn.

Cantrell pointed out the three men who leaned back on the corral, looking at Raider. "That boy in the cowhide hat is Easel Martin."

A slender man in clean clothes tipped his hat to Raider.

"They call me Ease. Where'd you find this giant, Mr. Cantrell?"

"Tinker's store."

"That where you found them squaws?" asked another man.

Cantrell glared and introduced him as Oat Weeks.

"Oat, short for Otis," said the second man.

He was stocky, big shoulders, flat face, reddish skin, pointed felt hat. "I'm partial to a squaw myself," Oat said. "Like 'em a whole lot better'n white women."

"Nobody's interested in your likes or dislikes, Weeks," Cantrell said. He pointed at the third man. "That's Johnny Dallas."

Raider knew that name. He looked down at the smartly dressed man who hid his face in the shadow of a black Stetson. When the dull eyes turned up to regard the big man from Arkansas, Raider wondered if it could be the same man. The face looked gaunt, older than he remembered. Thin mustache, dark, weathered skin. Very thin hands, almost brittle looking.

Dallas was their top gun hand. Raider knew from the way the others acted toward him. Even Cantrell seemed a mite too respectful of the man who dressed more like a gambler than a gunfighter.

"He's a big one all right," Dallas said cooly. "Can he shoot?"

Raider decided it was time to speak up. He kept wishing he had been given time to put on some sort of disguise. Dallas didn't seem to recognize him. Maybe it was only the same name.

"I killed a boy name o' Johnny Dallas," Raider said. "Had it out with 'im in some saloon in Oklahoma. Or was it Texas?"

"You done me a favor," Dallas replied without much emotion. "I heard there was a little wolverine usin' my name. Wasn't he ridin' with some rustlers?"

Raider nodded. "He's ridin' with the angels, now."

"More like demons, if you get my drift," Dallas offered.

Raider saw it. The acceptance. Talk of killing. Hired on by the same man. Cantrell was watching them to see how it would go. Dallas didn't want to go through any challenges. Raider had to feel the same way.

Ease glanced up at the big man. "What's your name, buddy?"

"Ray, Ray Thornton."

Oat pointed to Raider's mount. "You ain't interested in sellin' that bay, are you?"

Raider shrugged. "We could talk 'bout it."

Cantrell turned his horse toward the main house. "I'll leave y'all to your business." He pointed to a bunkhouse up on a rise behind some stables. "Find yourself a bed. Don't worry none about the rest of 'em. Once word gets round that you whipped Lockett, nobody'll be wantin' to try you."

With that, Cantrell rode off toward a two-story house that gleamed white with a fresh coat of paint. The yard was neatly raked and a vegetable garden grew to one side of the house. Hills in the back, with forests and mountains beyond, were outlined against the sunset. Summer flowers poked through every available piece of turf.

"This is a right purty place," Raider said.

Oat was gawking at him. "You really take ol' Lockett, Ray?"

Raider climbed down off the mare, tipping back his hat, trying to be modest. "Reckon I did."

Dallas glared at him, striking a match to light the end of a hand-rolled cigarillo. "You don't look the worse for wear."

Ease was also gawking. "No, he don't."

Raider stretched and grimaced. "Lockett got in 'is licks."

"He try to knife you?" Oat asked.

"He tried. Mr. Cantrell broke it up. He's a good man."

Ease and Oat nodded.

Dallas had his eyes on the redwood handle of Raider's Peacemaker. "Nice Colt." He drew back his coat, revealing the wooden butt of another big Colt, just like Raider's. "Pine," he said. "I like it better than ivory or pearl. Gives a better grip."

Raider nodded. "I'm partial to a wooden grip myself. I carved these when I was up Oregon way. Lot o' redwood there."

Ease nodded. "I heard tell Oregon is a fine place."

"Too many mosquitos," Raider replied. "Too much rain."

Oat had fixed on the mare. "Mind if I take her for a roll?"

Raider handed him the reins. "Don't know if I'd sell 'er though. The price'd have t' be right."

Oat swung into the saddle and started off at a walk. Ease followed him on foot. "We'll put your stuff in the bunkhouse," Oat called back over his shoulder.

Raider watched them go. "Friendly, ain't they?"

"They're dangerous," Dallas said quickly.

Raider glared at the slick gunman. "How so?"

"Local fools. They can shoot all right, but they can't draw for beans. They claim to have killed people, but I doubt if they have. And even if they have, it wasn't in a toe-to-toe gunfight."

His voice was low, icy. He spoke like a man who was interested only in staying alive. Cautious, like a rattler on a patch of cold ground.

"How's 'bout showin' me round, Dallas?"

The gunfighter squared his shoulders. "I got to warn you, Thornton. Cantrell has got a bunch of amateurs working for him. Don't expect anyone here to cover your back in a fight."

"I thought Cantrell was hirin' up all the top guns round here."

Dallas drew hard on the cigarillo, exhaling into the breeze. "You and I are the only top guns within eight hundred miles of this place."

"How you know I'm a top gun?"

Dallas flinched and slapped his holster. His dark brown eyes grew wide. He had a sly smirk on his face.

Raider looked down to see the Colt in his hand. He had hardly been aware of drawing it. The big man spun it quickly back down into the holster.

"You're fast," Dallas said. "Maybe as fast as me."

"How'd you know I wouldn't shoot you, Dallas?"

The gunfighter laughed a bone-dry chuckle. "I didn't."

Raider laughed with him. "I reckon I need some bunk time if I'm fallin' for parlor tricks like that one."

Dallas gestured toward the white house. "Why don't you demand that Cantrell let you sleep in the main house? I have a room upstairs."

Raider squinted at the gunman. "That right?"

"He's scared of you," Dallas said.

"He seemed pretty quick with a gun."

Dallas shrugged. "Not quick enough."

Raider figured the bunkhouse was good enough for him. "I'm gonna sleep there t'night. I ain't in the mood for arguin' with Cantrell."

Besides, being in the bunkhouse might give him a little more freedom of movement. He planned to do some night riding, looking around after dark. Learn the territory. Locate any possible places to hide cattle. Locate the lair of Red Dog. He had his work cut out for him.

As they walked toward the bunkhouse, Raider kept his eyes open. He saw a blacksmith at work in the stable, shoeing horses for the remuda. A trail drive used a lot of horses. How far would Cantrell be taking his cows?

The house was alive with the voices of the Feather sisters, who were taking over the kitchen, ousting an old woman who would be condemned to a life of toting water and sweeping floors now that the Cheyenne terrors had arrived. Raider was glad to be rid of them, although he wouldn't have minded a few more minutes alone with Bright Feather.

"Squaws," Johnny Dallas slurred with contempt. "They're bad luck. And they'll just cause trouble. As if Cantrell doesn't have worries enough."

"Some say he's stealin' cows from Three Forks," Raider offered.

Dallas shook his head. "He makes the wranglers cut out the Three Forks steers. Then they drive 'em back north. Mac Wilson should return the favor, but instead he accuses Cantrell of rustling."

"Thought Red Dog was the rustler?"

"You've heard of him too?" Dallas asked.

Raider said the name was all over the territory. Then he offered the popular notion that Red Dog was either working for Cantrell, or was Cantrell in disguise. This only brought a dry smirk to the gunslinger's thin lips.

"Where're all the hands?" Raider asked to change the subject.

"In the second turn of the roundup. They're ranging all the way to the forests. Going to give some beef to the government, for the Indians. The Crow just settled up there, you know."

Raider nodded. "Gonna be some herd."

"I'll move on before the drive begins."

Raider eyed the dapper shootist. "Can't figure out what a boy like you is doin' up in these parts. You seem more suited to a place like Denver."

"There are too many laws in Denver," was the cryptic reply.

Dallas stopped and pointed to the bunkhouse. "Just follow the path. I'll speak with Cantrell."

"I wouldn't mind sleepin' in the house sooner or later," the big man replied. "Tonight this'll be just fine."

"Watch your back, Thornton. And watch mine too if you get a chance."

Raider grinned, extending his hand. "If you'll return the favor."

Dallas's brittle hands were stronger than they looked. He shook with Raider and started back toward the house. He was smooth. Something struck Raider suddenly—it had all been smooth, like he was being soaped. Did they just want to make the new hand welcome? Or were they on to him?

"Hey, Ray! Up here!"

Oat was waving from the bunkhouse. Raider walked on up to meet him. At the crest of the rise, he looked out over the plain. The fading light shimmered over the wildflowers and the breezes were cool and scented by blossoms. If Oat hadn't started in on him, he might have enjoyed the view.

"Ray, I really like this mare."

Raider turned back to see that the horse had been stripped of his saddle and the rest of his gear.

"Don't get riled," Oat said quickly. "Ease took your stuff upstairs. There's a loft up there. You can have it."

"He the kind to take somethin' ain't his?"

Before Oat could reply, Ease came out of the bunkhouse. "Hey, there, Ray. Got it all fixed for you upstairs. Don't look mean at me, I didn't go through your saddlebags."

Raider shook his head. "Don't usually like nobody handlin' my goods, but I'll overlook it this time, since you boys is bein' so hospitable."

"Bein' what?" Ease asked.

"Shut up, Ease," Oat said. "I'm talkin' business with Ray about buyin' this mare. How about it, big man?"

Raider sighed, deciding that these two yokels were as stupid as they seemed. They weren't bad men, just a little slow. It might do him well to sell the mare and get in good with them.

"What will I ride if I sell her to you, Oat?"

The stocky gunhand tipped back his floppy hat. "Well, I been ridin' this big stallion. Roan, about nineteen hands high. He's too much for me, but you oughtta be able to handle him."

That sounded like a good swap, but Raider wanted to play it out a little more. "Look here, Oat, I got 'bout eighty dollars in that mare. How I know this stallion is good 'nough?"

Oat said he'd be right back and broke into a run.

Raider tried to stop him, but he was determined to make the trade.

"That stallion is a good one," Ease said in defense of his friend. "He's just too rough for Oat."

"I'm sure he is, Ease. I'm sure he is."

Raider turned his black irises toward the horizon again. It was bumpy, hilly land. Some trees, but mostly deep grasses and wildflowers. The closer you got to the forests in the west, the more uneven the land became. And in the foothills of the Rockies, there were thousands of ravines and crevices to hide in.

"It ain't hard to see why this is called the big country," Raider offered. "Plenty o' places for a man like Red Dog t' hide."

"Yeah, I reckon."

Raider wheeled toward Ease. "You don't seem too scared o' him."

Ease shrugged. "Ain't never done nothin' t' me. I hunted him at times, but I can't say I ever seen him."

Even Ease was playing it cool.

He turned back to the west. A dot that looked like a group of ants was moving over a hill and down into the depression between the first crest and the second rise. Cows coming in for the roundup. Raider wanted to get a look at them, to see what brands they wore. Something still did not feel right about the Delta Plain Cattle Company. He needed to get as much information as quickly as he could and then clear out.

"Here comes Oat."

The stocky man rushed up the hill, pulling the stallion behind him. "He's got fresh shoes," he huffed and puffed. "Look at him. I ain't seen a finer horse lately."

Raider studied the roan with mock skepticism in his manner. "I don't know, Oat. You sure this is your horse t' trade?"

"Ain't part o' Cantrell's remuda. Is it Ease?"

"No, it ain't part o' Cantrell's remuda."

A couple of real wizards, Raider thought. Maybe they were not as dumb as they seemed. He couldn't rule out that possibility.

"All right," Oat said finally. "I'll throw in ten bucks."

Raider nodded. "You're on, Oat. Now how 'bout takin' these animals down while I get some shut-eye?"

"You mean it?"

"I do."

Oat ran off for the stable, leading the mare and the stallion. Ease went with him, trailing like a little brother. They'd make good husbands for the Feather Sisters, although Raider figured Bright Feather would eat them both alive.

He turned once more to look at the plain.

It seemed so peaceful. A light breeze and a brilliant sunset. He could also hear the cows that came up over the second rise, making for one of the holding pens. Why would Cantrell steal cattle if he had so many already? Unless theft was his main source of livestock.

He went into the bunkhouse, which smelled better than most bunkhouses he had been in. His loft was even better. There was a real bed made from tanned hides and pine logs. His gear was stacked neatly by the wall.

Raider stretched out on the bed, putting his Colt on his stomach, gripping the redwood handle. He closed his eyes, but found that he suddenly could not sleep. His mind was going, sizing up everything he had seen. That same nagging feeling would not go away.

Was it that he was afraid of Cantrell and his crew?

No. He *wasn't* scared of them. That was the problem. Even Johnny Dallas, Cantrell's top gun, had not seemed as dangerous as could be expected at the beginning's of a range war. On second thought, Dallas seemed like he was on the skids, fleeing to the north country after too many sins in the southern territories. A gunslinger's trespasses always drove him into rough country sooner or later.

Raider exhaled, listening to the bawling cows in the distance. Whether he liked it or not, he was now the top gun for Cantrell and the Delta Plain. That distinction might put him in some tight places in a hurry. He lay on the bed, trying to sort it all out in his head. Gradually, he lost interest in solutions and drifted off into an uneasy slumber.

Raider heard her scratching. She was crying too. Her face was right in front of him. She reached out to him.

Raider reached back. He was young again and she was there. He did not know how it could have happened, but there he was, back in Wyoming with the girl from Cheyenne. Her eyes were blue and her hair brown, her smile as youthful as it had been then.

But her smile vanished and he saw another face, a darker face. She had a knife and was digging at something. It wasn't Thalia at all, but the pointed face of a savage.

Raider opened his eyes and sat up on the bed.

The girl with the knife was coming through the small window of the loft.

He thumbed back the Peacemaker, lifting it from his belly. "I'll kill you!" he said in a whisper.

"Shh!" the girl said. "It's me. Bright Feather."

Raider kept his Colt leveled at the girl. As the matters at hand came back to him, he lowered the weapon, realizing where he was. Bright Feather got through the window and sat down next to him on the bed.

"Listen!" she said in a low voice.

Raider heard laughter downstairs. The bunkhouse was full of men. They were probably all waiting to meet the man who had bested Lockett, their moose. He'd have to show himself sooner or later.

Bright Feather put her hand on his thigh. "They're talking about you in the main house."

Raider looked at her. "What are they sayin'?"

She glanced away. "I don't think they know you're a Pinkerton."

He grabbed her shoulders. "Did you tell 'em?"

"Nooo," she whined. "You're hurting me."

He let her go. "Don't go runnin' your mouth. Hell, come t' think of it, Tinker also knows who I really am."

"Maybe he won't come back for a while," Bright Feather said.

Raider stood up, reaching for his holster. "Maybe."

Bright Feather reclined on the bed. "I won't tell anybody."

"You better not."

She began to pull up her dress. "Do you have to go right now?"

He looked out the window. "I want t' ride t'night. I want t' see if I can find Red Dog. Are they talkin' 'bout Red Dog in the main house?"

"I don't know."

He turned back to see her dark legs on the bed. She had lifted her dress abover her stomach. The black wedge between her thighs was just a shadow. Raider felt the bothersome stirring.

"I ain't got time, woman."

"Oh, come on. If you don't, you'll wish you had."

That was true enough. He scowled at her. "I thought you was gonna marry Cantrell. Or did you think you'd find a better deal with me?"

"Shut your mouth!" she snapped. "I ain't gonna marry Cantrell. Little Bright Feather is gonna marry him."

"Ain't she too young?"

The Cheyenne girl shrugged. "Not to be married. I was married at that age. Marriage is fine. But she has to stay a virgin till then."

The laughter rose from downstairs. Raider listened carefully to a voice that belonged to Lockett. Like an eager child, Lockett was telling the tale of his own whipping, to set the record straight and to be the center of attention for a while. He was telling it close to the truth too, although he was making Raider sound a lot meaner than he actually was.

"You did break his back," Bright Feather said.

Raider stepped toward the bed, sliding next to her. "No need t' interrupt him in the middle o' his story."

Her breath quickened. "Oh, I want that big thing."

She didn't even kiss him. Her hands worked the buttons of his fly, freeing his massive erection. When it was in her hands, she jerked him for a few seconds before she straddled his crotch.

Bright Feather guided his prickhead to the opening of her vagina.

Slowly she sat down on him, filling herself in a gradual motion.

Raider let her stay on top for a while. She was good with those little hips working up and down. She seemed to straddle him like a grasshopper, rising and falling on her nubile legs.

"Damn, that feels good," she said through clenched teeth.

Raider cupped her tight ass. "You've had enough fun," he told her. "Now I'm gonna be on top."

He reversed their position without coming out of her.

Their bodies rocked, two motions blending finally into one. Raider came deep, plunging himself inside her. Bright Feather arched her back, gasping with her own climactic release. When he tried to pull out, she stopped him.

"Leave it in," she whispered. "Leave it in just a few more seconds."

"I ain't got time t' . . ."

She sank her fingernails into his buttocks. "I said leave it in."

Her cunt made a squishy sound as it tightened.

He tried again to get off her.

"I'll tell everyone you're a Pinkerton," she teased. "You better leave it where I say to leave it."

She did something with her finger that made him hard again.

Raider repeated his hip motion, driving both of them into a second climax. Bright Feather seemed satisfied, so he climbed off her, sitting on the edge of the bed. The girl slid up beside him.

"Here," she said, "let me clean you up."

Using a fold of her calico dress, she wiped his cock and shoved it into his pants, fixing the buttons.

"You better get back before you're missed," Raider said.

She pulled down the dress. "We're sleeping in back. On the porch with the old woman."

"Cantrell wouldn't give you a room?"

"We didn't want one," Bright Feather replied. "Not until he marries Little Bright Feather. We want that ring on her finger."

"Good luck."

She started for the window. "Don't worry. Your secret is safe with me. I'll be back to see you."

"Not t'night," he warned. "I'll be in the saddle till t'morrow mornin'."

Bright Feather looked at the sky. "You should have a good moon. It won't come up for a while, though."

"Git on outta here, woman. And keep your yap shut."

"Screw you, cowboy."

Before he could reply, she was through the window and gone.

Raider listened as Lockett wrapped up his tale. The big man took a deep breath. He had to think about being recognized again. What if he had crossed one of the cowboys somewhere? It didn't even have to be in the line of duty. Raider was known to bust a few heads when he was having a good time. Women, liquor, and gambling often helped to kindle a good whorehouse brawl. Nothing dangerous, just some Saturday night fun.

His stomach did a somersault, trying to come out through his ribs. Word got around on the plain, even if it did seem impossible. How long before someone mentioned the Pinkerton who had been hired by the territorial governor's office? How long before somebody put it all together?

Raider strapped on his holster, tying it low like a gunslinger. He had to act like the cock of the walk. As top fist and top gun, he was going to be expected to fulfill certain requirements that went with the image. He might even have to draw down with somebody in a real gunfight.

As he started down the stairs, he told himself to be quick about it. Just meet the men and get it over with. If it came to facing the bore of a hot iron Colt, he'd just have to make sure he was a little faster.

CHAPTER EIGHT

Summer came quickly to Chicago, chasing away the late spring chill, replacing the inclement weather with days so fine that a man was loath to sit at his desk and work.

William Wagner, however, was not a man to readily give in to the comforts of a sunny afternoon. There was always work to be done around the Pinkerton agency. Case files had to be closed, paperwork caught up on, agents to be directed to their various investigations. And naturally, at some time or other during the workday, Wagner's thoughts would turn to Raider. He'd muse for a moment, as he did with all his agents, and then move on. Raider wasn't somebody to put his mind at ease.

Take for instance, Raider's current plight. No one really knew where he was or what he was doing. Had he caught the man he was chasing? Even if he had, he might be in some whorehouse, wasting precious time while his prisoner was lashed to the hitching post outside. He would be drinking too, something that was not permitted on duty. None of the drinking and whoring would be mentioned in his report—if he filed a report at all.

Wagner tossed the matter aside until Allan Pinkerton burst through the door with a combustible expression on his face. "William, my lad, I need your counsel in my office at once."

Wagner rose and followed his supervisor, somewhat glad to be relieved of his routine duties. Pinkerton never exuded such energy unless something interesting was afoot. The big Scotsman plopped behind his desk and began to sort through a sheaf of papers.

"Nothin' like a summer day to get the blood flowin'," he said loudly, wiping sweat from his brow.

Wagner nodded in agreement, wondering if there really was anything important to discuss.

Pinkerton lifted something from the clutter. "Here, William. Read this. See what you make of it."

Wagner took the newspaper clipping from him. It was a notice from a weekly paper in Billings, Montana. The publication was set in a crude type and the spelling was atrocious, but the message was clear. The headline over the story read: "Range War Threat in E. Territory Sets Ranchers Ablaze."

"This is the report we've been waiting for," Pinkerton said.

Wagner looked up suddenly. "Yes, they requested a team of agents and we sent them Raider. Someone to deal with this Red Dog."

Pinkerton handed him another piece of paper, a telegram from Helena. "It took a while to get here, but we finally got confirmation."

Wagner read the communique that established Raider's capture of Johnson Selks. It also said that Raider was on his way to deal with the trouble in the eastern territory. Wagner sighed and reread the newspaper clipping.

Pinkerton watched him, waiting for a response.

His associate finally lifted his head. "Do you think there's any truth to the report that the ranchers are hiring top guns?"

Pinkerton shrugged. "Maybe. But that's just a small town journal tryin' to interest its readers."

"True. But I've no doubt that the sense of it is valid, even if the particulars are exaggerated."

The big Scotsman rose from his chair and went to study his map of the western territories. "Right here. Where these three rivers come together. Some say it's pretty country. Have you ever seen it, William?"

Wagner nodded. "Yes. A few times, when I was younger. It can be harsh territory, especially in winter."

Pinkerton rubbed his chin, turning away. "Darn me. I don't know what to do. Raider's on his own with no backup. That marshal ain't worth two hoots in Hell to him."

Wagner chortled nervously. "Raider wouldn't work with him if he offered to help. You know he works alone."

"Aye."

It was the same old argument about the big man from Arkansas. Could he handle the trouble by himself? Sometimes Wagner was tempted to force a partner on him under threat of termination. He often wondered if it had been a mistake to let him work solo. His former partner had always tempered Raider, keeping him somewhat under control.

"Maybe we should pull him out," Wagner offered. "Just let the Montana territorial government take care of it."

"What little government there is couldn't raise a barn without borrowin' a crew from another territory," Pinkerton replied. "Besides, I think Raider has enough sense to ask for a hand or to get out if the situation gets to be too much for him."

Wagner held his tongue, unable to voice similar optimism. He had a vision of Raider with a flaming gun, shooting until his last bullet was gone, facing insurmountable odds without a prayer of victory. Raider would rather die than give up. In some men such tenacity would be considered an asset, but in Raider it was probably the thing that would get him killed.

"What is your official word?" Pinkerton asked.

Wagner sighed. "The three choices are: one, send in help; two, pull him out of there; three, leave him alone."

"And what's your vote?"

Wagner thought about it a while. "Well, if we send help, it might reveal any cover that Raider has established. That could get him killed."

"Aye."

"If we pull him out, he'll be angry at us, may even quit if he's got his back up enough."

"No doubt."

"So, I suppose the only thing to do is to let him be," Wagner said, "Just wait for word to trickle back to us."

Pinkerton grinned. "So you vote for number three?"

Wagner shrugged. "What choice do I have?"

"I hope we don't regret it, William."

Wagner did not think of it in terms of regret. "I do have to say this, sir."

"I'm listenin'."

"Since we're only sending one man in on this case, I'm glad it's Raider. I wouldn't dare send one of our other agents on a mission of this nature. I can't think of anyone else who might be able to handle it alone."

Pinkerton agreed. He directed Wagner to get word to several other operatives, to tell them to be ready in case Raider needed some backup. Wagner went back to his desk.

He considered which agents to inform of the situation, but finally decided to delay Pinkerton's ruling. If he contacted the other men right away, they might go barreling straight into Raider's mess and get him hurt. There was no way to know what was going on in southeastern Montana, so Wagner could really do very little but wait.

Whatever the situation, Wagner was sure of one thing: if there was big trouble in the Montana cattle country, Raider was right in the middle of it.

And the reckless, hell-bent Pinkerton from Arkansas had to deal with it on his own.

CHAPTER NINE

Raider hadn't even reached the bottom of the stairs before a man cried out, "You son of a bitch."

The man reached for his pistol, glaring hatefully at the big Pinkerton.

All of the other hands dived for the floor, fearing a stray bullet in the crossfire.

Raider drew his Peacemaker, firing two shots before the man could get his old, rusty Colt out of the holster.

The man gulped for air, stumbling forward, blood gushing from the holes in his chest. He walked straight for Raider, his eyes wide with the impending knowledge of death. His voice creaked one last syllable.

"Rai . . . Rai . . ."

He fell flat on the floor, dropping his gun beside him. Blood pooled beneath him, oozing into the cracks between the floorboards. The other hands came slowly back to life, jockeying for position to get a look at the body.

Oat Weeks stepped over the dead man. "Better get him outside before he mucks up the floor."

Somebody suggested that they get the old woman to doctor the man who lay bleeding in their bunkhouse.

Ease Martin shook his head. "Only thing he's gonna need is an undertaker. Here, better roll him over."

Raider stood on the bottom step, the smoking Colt still in his hand. His black eyes roved around the bunkhouse, seeing if anyone else wanted some hot lead. There were no takers. He kept the Colt ready, just in case.

Ease turned the body over. "Heart shots, both of them."

"Weren't no way he could miss from that range," someone suggested.

Raider looked at the man who had said it. He was a little runt, rat-faced and slit-eyed. One of the men called him Sooty, probably because his face had never been washed.

Sooty didn't seem to share the fear that the other men had of Raider. "How come that dead one to draw down on you?"

Raider shrugged, looking at the deceased cowboy's face. "Don't know. I think I seen 'im before. What's his name?"

"Myers," Oat Weeks replied. "Jimmy Myers."

Raider thought hard about it. Where had he seen the man before? If he could remember, he might be able to make up a plausible story. Suddenly it hit him. Myers had been part of a gang he had sent to prison in Wyoming. If he was quick on his feet . . .

"Rock Springs," he said.

Oat's eyes narrowed. "The prison in Wyoming?"

Raider nodded. "Did some time there with this boy. He crossed me an' I took 'im t' task. Said he'd get even with me. I reckon he tried."

This did not seem good enough for Sooty. "I heard him talk about Rock Springs. Said some Pinkerton sent him there. Said that was who he wanted to get even with. Besides, he called Ray by name. Did it afore he died."

They all turned their eyes on Raider.

Oat Weeks nodded. "He was always talkin' about that Pinkerton. Man name of Doc Weatherbee. Couldn't remember the other one. Said there was two of them sent him to prison."

Raider shook his head. "Well, I heard 'im talk about the same men. I know how he felt, cause it was a Pinkerton sent me t' the same place. Boy name of Stokes."

Ease Martin glared at the big man. "How long was you in Rock Springs?"

Raider shrugged. "Two years, but that was a while back."

"Got a guard there," Sooty challenged. "A big, fat-back ape. If you'd done time like you said, you'd know that guard."

Raider grinned from ear to ear because he knew the name they wanted: "Bull Watson," he said. "Had many a run-in with 'im."

This seemed to satisfy everyone but Sooty.

"I still say Jimmy wouldn't've drawed down on nobody but

somebody that done him wrong!" the dirty man declared.

Raider decided to put an end to Sooty's carping. He strode a few steps toward the man and gave him a long, hateful look. Sooty backed off, shaking like a leaf in a strong wind.

"You want to try me the way Myers did?" Raider asked.

Spittle dribbled out between the man's brown lips. "Ain't got no truck with you."

"Then keep your mouth shut."

If the hands of the Delta Plain wanted to press the issue, they could have done so easily. There were twenty of them, and only four bullets left in Raider's Colt. But no one wanted to be among the four that died before the others got the big man.

Raider swung back to look at the corpse. "Get him outta here."

Ease and Oat started to drag the bulk toward the front door.

"Lift him," someone said. "You're dragging a trail all the way to the door. Nobody wants to clean up that blood."

Raider stopped them. "Now listen up, all o' you. I hired on here with Mr. Cantrell t' see some action. He's havin' trouble with this Red Dog. I aim t' help 'im. Now anybody else wants t' try me, do it now. If you want t' shoot me, try it head on. 'Cause you won't have a chance if you try to shoot me in the back. Understood?"

Everybody nodded, including the reluctant Sooty.

Raider was turning to go back up the stairs when the door swung open.

Johnny Dallas stood on the threshold with his Peacemaker drawn. He looked at Raider, then at the body. After lowering the Colt, he stepped into the bunkhouse and nudged the corpse with the toe of his boot.

"Dead as a doornail," offered Oat Weeks.

Dallas looked up at Raider. "What happened, big man?"

"Had some trouble with this boy back in Rock Springs," Raider replied. "Reckon he thought he could get even."

A dry smile stretched across Dallas's thin lips. "Y'all see this," he said to the crew. "That big 'un there ain't nobody to mess with. Is he, Lockett?"

The fat galoot had been hanging back in the shadows. Raider anticipated trouble, but instead, Lockett spoke in his behalf. "No, sir, Mr. Dallas. This big 'un ain't one t' be messed with."

Sooty had other ideas, like he could speak more freely with another gun to back him up. "This boy says he's goin' after Red Dog, Mr. Dallas. Claims he hired on to catch that thievin' half-breed."

A curious expression crossed over the gunfighter's thin face. He motioned with his Colt. "Can I see you outside, Thornton?"

Raider hesitated for a second, until he remembered that Thornton was his alias. He followed Dallas outside, expecting more complications. When they were alone in the shadows, Dallas gave him a pat on the back.

"Can't blame you for shootin' Myers," the gunslinger offered. "He was trouble from the git go. Cantrell was ready to fire him anyway. Looks like you saved him the trouble."

Again he was smooth, too slippery like a Missouri River eel.

Raider nodded. "Yeah, well, it had t' be done."

They were silent for a moment, as Oat and Ease dragged the body out of the bunkhouse.

"Bury him on the other side of the hill," Dallas ordered. "And cover him with rocks so the coyotes can't get to him!"

When they were gone, he turned back to Raider. "That true, what you said about findin' Red Dog?"

The big man decided to test the waters. "If that's what Cantrell wants, I'm ready t' get the job done."

The sly smile returned to the dapper shootist's lips. "Cantrell said to give you free range. Said you can take any horse you want. Though I heard you traded for the big roan."

"That I did."

"All right," Dallas replied. "Go on. Do what you have to. Day or night. It don't matter. If you think you can find Red Dog, have at it."

That said, the oily gunfighter started to walk back toward the main house.

"Dallas!"

The gunman turned back to face him. "Yes?"

"You're welcome t' come along if you want," Raider offered.

A laugh from Dallas. "No thanks. I'll tend the home fires. If you corner him, give me a holler."

He wheeled and disappeared into the shadows.

Too smooth, Raider thought again. They were giving him a free hand. Or were they? He had seen smarter setups. Maybe this was one of them.

Back inside the bunkhouse, Raider asked for volunteers to help look for Red Dog. There were no takers. When pressed, Lockett replied that they were there to protect the herd, not look for ghosts.

"You sayin' Red Dog ain't real?" Raider challenged.

But there was no reply, only a hangdog look from Lockett.

Raider went back upstairs to get his gear. When he came down, the men were talking vociferously. They stopped when they saw him. He stared at them for a moment and then strode out into the night.

When he was outside, he could hear them talking again and he was almost sure that he was the main topic of conversation.

Bright Feather had been right about one thing. It was a good night for the moon. As Raider strode toward the stable, the round, silver orb came up out of the east, lighting the rolling plain.

The blacksmith had his mount ready. Raider saddled the roan and then went through his saddlebags. No harm done. Everything was intact. Why did he feel so cautious?

He looked at the smithy. "What's goin' on round here, hoss?"

The man smiled. "I just shoe 'em, big man. Don't pay much attention to anything else."

"Ever'body seems to be in the dark round here," Raider muttered.

The smitty pointed to the sky. "Not tonight."

The roan bucked a little when Raider mounted up, but it didn't take long for the big man to establish who was boss. When the stallion settled down, Raider spurred it to the north. He drove hard for the crest of a ridge where he could look back over the entire Delta Plain spread.

There was lots of land in Montana. Raider wondered if it would ever be settled like some of the other states and territories. Hell, California and Texas were crowded compared to Montana. You couldn't ride ten miles in Texas without seeing somebody, unless you worked hard at it. In California it was even worse.

Raider sighed, listening to the sound of the cattle below. The night was so clear and cool, the breeze so steady, that he could smell them. It seemed improbable that anyone could have trouble in such a place. Except for seeing the rustlers taking the cattle south, there had been very little evidence that anything was wrong at all.

He lifted his gun hand, which was shaking, a reaction to killing the man. He hadn't enjoyed it and, in fact, it had happened so fast that the discomfort of the shooting had waited to settle in on him. But there was no time to dwell on the poor bastard who was being laid in his grave. Raider turned the roan off the ridge and continued north.

Cantrell had claimed to chase Red Dog to the north. Raider figured to prove him right or wrong. As he rode, something continued to bother him. He finally realized that he was worried about proving Cantrell wrong. He had come to like the red-haired man and the crew of the Delta Plain. But he had to put that out of his mind, in case Cantrell really was working with Red Dog.

The country got rougher after he crossed the Powder River. A long, high ridge ran to his left, going north as far as he could see in the moonlight. He stopped by the river, letting the roan drink. He listened in the night air but could hear nothing beyond the babbling of the water.

Suddenly he felt sort of stupid, as if he had done exactly as someone had wanted him to do. No wonder Cantrell had made it so easy for him to go hunting in the darkness. He probably knew that Raider wasn't going to find a damn thing.

Raider was turning the roan south when he heard the riders coming. This was it, he thought. Cantrell and his men were coming to finish him. They weren't far away. Coming from the east. They had swung around, or maybe they had been waiting for him all along.

He glanced back toward the ridge. There were plenty of rocks he could hide in. He had his rifle and his Colt. Maybe he could hold them off. He listened again to the hooves—five or six horses.

Raider guided the roan toward the ridge, dismounting when he reached the rocks. He hid the stallion behind a rock and hobbled it so it wouldn't stray. Then he moved in the moonlight, slipping away from the stallion in case it made a sound and betrayed his position.

The riders pounded up to the river. Raider could hear them as they watered their mounts. He peered over a rock, his Winchester in his hand. If they started toward him, tracking in the moonglow, he planned to shoot quickly and get as many as he could before they found cover. Six of them. Not bad odds if he could plug three or four of them immediately.

His black eyes peered down the sight of the Winchester, fixing the lead rider as the first target. Just a little closer. His finger tightened on the trigger. But then the lead rider waved his hand and the men started north, driving away from him.

He lowered the rifle. "Son of a bitch."

The hooves pounded along the ridge, the sound growing fainter as they disappeared into the night.

Raider got up, hurrying back to the stallion. He had fully expected a fight, an ambush. Maybe the riders had just missed his trail. Even a comanche had trouble tracking in the dark.

He guided the roan out of the rocks and swung into the saddle. He looked south, wondering if there was another group of men who might come after him. If he rode back, maybe he would meet them. But then his curiosity got the better of him. He had to ride north, to see what the other men were after.

They weren't hard to track. Even on the rocky ground there was enough dust to mark their trail. He could also hear them, even though he was hanging back far enough that he could not be seen or heard. They rode hard for what seemed like a couple of hours. Raider lifted his eyes to the moon once in a while to confirm the passage of time.

He kept wondering how long they would follow the ridge. He had expected the rise to disappear, but instead it only got higher, angling to the northwest. The riders held steady, paralleling the rise without once deviating from the course. If they were after him, they had given him credit for covering more territory than he had.

And then, before he realized it, they were gone.

The riders had just disappeared ahead of him. He rode past their dust into the clear air. At first, he thought he was seeing things. But he doubled back to check their tracks and found the place where the hoofprints ended.

He looked toward the ridge to his left. They had turned off into the rocks, all six of them. There was a narrow path that seemed to lead straight to a dead end at the ledge of the ridge.

Raider ducked low all of a sudden, expecting shots from the ambush. But nothing happened. He stayed low, listening for sounds of movement.

The roan snorted.

"Where are they boy?"

Raider lifted his head into the breeze. Something odd struck him. It was the smell. He detected the odor of cattle on the breeze. But that was it. No sounds, no movement.

"Damn."

He considered riding back to the Delta Plain to get some backup. Maybe Oat Weeks and Ease Martin could help him. But that might not work. By the time he reached the bunkhouse, the men in the rocks could be gone—if, even now, they were still there. Besides, maybe the riders were from the Delta Plain, in which case no one would be ready to lend a hand.

So he found a place to hide the roan and started into the rocks on foot. The path the men had followed widened as it wound up toward the ridge. The smell of cattle became stronger as he drew closer to the rise. He also heard bawling and the clicking of horns.

How the hell could they hide cows in the rocks?

He hesitated beside a big rock, listening. Shod hooves clopped on the trail. A horseman was coming his way. Raider drew back into the shadows, clutching the Winchester to his chest.

There were two of them, passing right by him. He managed to pick up a few snatches of their conversation. The voices did not sound familiar, but there was one name that did strike a chord.

"I don't like it," one of them said.

"Yeah, but Red Dog says that's the deal. Come on, we got to get back and take care of it."

They rode on out of the rocks and drove back to the east.

Raider let out the breath that he had been holding. So Red Dog was real. Or at least real enough to those boys.

The smell of the cattle would not let him be. He had to get back into the rocks and see what was there. But how? If he stayed low on the trail, the others might eventually spot him. There was only one thing to do: climb.

It was difficult in the dark. He had to take each step slowly, groping for purchase. Eventually he found a path up the ledge. He had to pause halfway to rest. As he gazed to the south, he saw the faint glow of the Delta Plain lights. Due west, another set of lights shimmered more brightly. Was that the Three Forks spread? Had he come that far north?

Maybe the boys who rode past him on the trail were from the Three Forks spread. But why would they mention Red Dog? There was no reason to assume they were from Three Forks just because they had headed west.

He started climbing, spurred on by the smells and sounds of cattle. As he was nearing the summit of the ridge, he saw the clouds that were rolling down from the north. The wind picked up a little and the air suddenly felt charged with electricity.

Raider stood up on the crest of the rise, his eyes growing wide at the bizarre sight below him. It looked like a thousand devils, blue horns aglow in a box canyon. He had seen it before, but the spectacle was still enough to steal a man's breath.

St. Elmo's fire. He didn't know what caused it, but there it was. The cows' horns were glowing blue in the night. When the clouds pushed over the moon, the shine seemed even brighter.

The cows were spooky, but the tight corral of the box canyon kept them from stampeding. Raider took his black eyes away from the sight long enough to search for the men who had put the cattle in the secluded place. Where the hell were they? If the clouds hadn't blown in, he would have been able to see them in the moonlight.

"Damn it all."

He had to get closer. It was probably a dangerous thing to try, but he had to climb down the other side of the ridge. If he could hear them, maybe he could find out who was working with Red Dog.

As he started down, the rain came on. A hard, driving deluge wet the cows, dispersing the blue glow from their horns. Raider tried to keep going, but finally he had to huddle beneath a rocky ledge to stay out of the downpour. His eyes became heavy and he fought to stay awake. But in the blinding rain, he could not shake off the fatigue. He napped for a while, waking to the gruff sound of voices rising out of the canyon.

"I'm tellin' you, I don't think we should move yet, Red Dog. We want to take our time."

Raider leaned over, peering down into the box canyon. He could see two men. One was shorter than the other. The short man wore a broad Stetson. The taller one had long hair and a headband was wrapped around his skull.

The man with the headband was undoubtedly Red Dog. He didn't seem to be a Cheyenne, though. Even in the light of the low western moon, Raider could tell Red Dog was an Apache. What the hell was he doing so far north?

"I am boss!" the Indian insisted. "I say we move. Too many cows here now. We move!"

The man in the Stetson shook his head. "Don't make trouble, Red Dog. You're tough, but you ain't got nobody behind you. Don't press your luck."

This did not seem to mollify the big Apache, who grunted and moved away from the other man.

"You're gonna get your money and your guns, Red Dog," the Stetson man insisted. "But you got to wait like everyone else."

Raider nodded appreciatively. He had to give it to the Indian. Steal a few cows at a time, hide them, wait for the herd to grow. He wondered how many more pockets of cattle were hidden in the rocky reaches of the territory. And was Cantrell really behind it?

He watched Red Dog, who moved down to strew hay all

over the canyon. It might get tricky to feed a bunch of penned-up cattle. The smell was enough to gag a normal man. Raider still couldn't figure out why somebody would rustle steers when the country seemed to be full of them.

As he drew back into the rocks, he was aware of a purple glow in the sky behind him. The sun was starting to rise. He had been asleep for longer than he thought. He had to get out, to get back to . . . to who?

Maybe he could get word to the marshal, although that might not do any good. Junior Mays would raise a posse and back him up. But by the time that happened, word would be out and the rustlers could move their cows.

But those were worries for later. Right now he had to get out of the canyon and back to his mount. He started to move, keeping his eye on Red Dog as he fed the steers. Suddenly the Indian turned his head up and looked straight at Raider. The big man from Arkansas slunk back into the shadows, not sure if had been seen.

Red Dog went back to his chore, allowing Raider to move again. He went quietly to the top of the rise and started downward. It would be fully daylight soon. He wanted to get south before someone saw him.

As he climbed down, he heard the clopping of hooves again. Three men, including the one in the broad Stetson, rode slowly over the narrow trail. Raider wondered how difficult it had been to get the cows to move single file along the path. The intelligence of the plan made him wonder if Red Dog was the mastermind. The Apache's gruntings hardly seemed that of a smart man.

While the riders were spurring their mounts to the south, Raider continued his descent. He tried to be quiet, but something pushed him along, an urgency that had not been there before. He was considering a gamble: to ride into the Delta Plain and flat out confront Cantrell with his knowledge of the hidden herd.

If he did that, Cantrell would have to show his hand. Maybe it wasn't so smart. Maybe he'd just wait and let the thing play itself out. Then he'd have time to get word to Junior Mays. They could form a solid plan to draw out Red Dog.

Of course, there was always the Three Forks spread. He could appeal to the ramrod there, the man named Wilson. Raider had only seen him once, with the woman. She had looked familiar, but Raider had decided she could not be the same girl he had known so many years ago.

As he reached the trail, Raider stopped, listening in the cool morning air. A few rocks rattled behind him. He waited with the Winchester ready, wondering if a mountain lion had smelled the cows and come down to take a look. But he did not hear any cougar's howling.

Still, he feared for his mount and started toward the spot where he had left the roan.

The stallion was snorting and rearing. Raider tried to calm him, but the roan wasn't having it.

"What the hell's wrong with you, boy?"

It could be the cougar. A cat didn't always howl when it was on the move. Raider untied the roan and started to lead it out of the rocks.

The stallion had no intention of settling down. It bucked as Raider tried to mount. Maybe if he led it further away from the ridge the roan would calm down.

"Come on, you lame-brained bag of guts."

Horses were just like women sometimes. They'd go along just fine, no trouble. Then, just when you needed them to cooperate, they'd start more trouble than a pack of drunk cowboys.

Before Raider had walked ten feet, the roan reared and whinnied as if it had been bitten by a rattler.

But there was no snake. Only the man, who jumped from a high rock, falling straight for Raider. The big man saw him for a second, silhouetted against what was left of the moonlight. Then he was on top him and they were fighting for their lives.

CHAPTER TEN

Raider tried to move aside, but the man landed squarely on his chest, knocking him to the ground. The big man's breath left him with a single grunt. He was paralyzed for an instant, trying to gulp air through the pain in his gut. Then the man was hovering over him and he heard the clicking of a pistol as it was cocked.

"Red Dog, he don't like nobody spyin' on him," the man said. "Now you're gonna die."

The moment of hateful discourse was all Raider needed. He rolled, whipping his legs into the man's ankles. A burst of fire erupted as the pistol went off. The slug slammed next to Raider's head, missing him by several inches.

The stallion snorted and shied as Raider's assailant tumbled to the ground. Raider struggled to find the man's gun hand. The pistol went off again, but this time Raider had gripped the man's wrist. He beat the gun hand against the ground until the man dropped the weapon.

Raider reached for his own Colt. The man swung a fist into his face, knocking him on his back again. Raider tried to recover, but the man was on him, strong hands closing around his throat.

"If I can't shoot you, I'll choke you to death."

But the big man from Arkansas had other ideas. He lifted the Peacemaker from his holster and swung it hard into the side of the bushwhacker's head. The man grunted and fell to the side, holding his temple.

Raider jumped to his feet, thumbing the hammer of the Colt. "Hold it steady, boy. I'll drop you in a heartbeat, if you don't start answerin' a few questions for me."

"Red Dog!" the man cried. "Help me, Red Dog!"

His voice startled the roan, which was already spooky from the two shots that had been fired. The big animal snorted, slamming into Raider, causing him to lose his balance. It was all the man on the ground needed. He jumped up and tackled Raider around the legs.

Raider tried to hang onto the Colt as he went down, but it didn't do any good. The man grabbed Raider's gun hand and sank his teeth into his wrist. Raider screamed, letting go of the Colt.

His attacker tried to grab the big weapon, but Raider managed to get a hand on his throat, toppling him away from the Peacemaker.

They rolled around on the hard ground, wrestling under the nervous legs of the roan.

Raider managed to pin the man and hold him for a second.

"Who the hell are you?"

The man breathed heavily, trying to fill his lungs.

"Better tell me now . . . dammit!"

The roan danced nervously over them, kicking Raider in the middle of the back. When his reflexes made him reach for the pain, the man shoved Raider off him and leaped to his feet.

"Now we're gonna see who kills who," the man slurred.

Raider could hear him searching for the gun. He saw his silhouette against the purple sky in the east. The pain felt like somebody had sunk an ax into his spine. But he could still feel his legs. And he could still reach for the knife in his boot.

The man picked up Raider's Colt and cocked it. "Now you're a dead one."

Raider lifted the hunting knife from his boot.

"So long, lawman."

He hurled it at the shadow that stood over him.

His assailant screamed like a wolverine, grabbing his shoulder. Raider hoped the knife went deep. He hoped it had caught him in the heart.

As the bushwhacker screeched his agony, Raider scuffled to his feet. The pain in his back was bad, but he had felt worse. He heard the roan snorting again. If he could just reach the rifle scabbard and get his Winchester. That would do it.

He took two steps, only to have the bushwhacker slam the butt of the Colt into his stomach.

Raider buckled over, wanting to vomit.

The man grunted again as he pulled the knife from the wound in his shoulder. "You're gonna pay for that one, lawman."

Raider couldn't find the strength for anything else, so he simply spat in the general direction of the gunman.

The man laughed horribly. "Spittin' like a Texas horn-frog before the rattler eats him alive."

Raider felt stones beneath his fingers.

"Won't do you no good, boy."

The man cocked the Colt again.

Raider grabbed a handful of rocks.

"You're a dead man."

Raider flung the rocks but he missed the man entirely.

Again the bushwhacker began his laugh, but this time he didn't finish it. The rocks hit the roan in the backside, making the nervous stallion jump; then he reared, rising over the gunman who turned in time to see the roan's hooves falling down toward his face.

The dull sound might have been sickening to anyone else, but it was music to Raider's ears. Splitting skull. Flopping of a body to the ground. More hooves cracking bone as the maddened stallion trampled the man.

Raider lay motionless on the ground, half-expecting the man to get up and draw down on him again.

The roan whinnied, pawing the corpse with its foot.

Raider sat up and looked at the sky. It would be light enough to see the man pretty soon. He could go through his pockets too, maybe find a clue there. First he had to get to his feet.

"Damn," he said to the roan. "You almost kill me and then you save my life. I don't know whether to shoot you or kiss you."

Sometimes, when an animal killed a human being, it was put to death immediately. He wondered how the roan would behave now that it had drawn blood. He might have to shoot the stallion soon enough, but as it stood, he was going to give the horse a second chance.

"I won't tell nobody you kilt him if you don't." He chortled to himself.

He tried to stand up, but found the pain to be excrutiating. Then he remembered that Red Dog was still around and had probably heard the fracas. That thought encouraged him to get on his feet fast. A rush of fear always dulled the ache a little.

The round globe of the sun was peeking over the eastern horizon. Raider saw his Colt lying on the ground. He picked it up and dropped it in his holster. The roan snorted again, like he approved.

Lucky, the big man thought, that they had been in the rocks; otherwise the stallion might be halfway back to the Delta Plain by now.

Raider grabbed the horse's reins, steadying him. He glanced back at the body of the dead man. The right side of his skull had collapsed under the force of the stallion's hooves.

He didn't feel like going through the man's pockets, but it had to be done. When he saw the deep wound in the man's shoulder, Raider remembered his hunting knife. He searched for the blade until he found it nearby, stained with crimson. The sun was bright enough to illuminate the rocks now. Raider figured he didn't have any more excuses to delay his search of the dead man's body. There was no way around it.

Unless he could take the man back to Delta Plain. Maybe somebody would recognize him. Raider shook his head. He had been careless in letting the man get the drop on him. Six riders had gone into the hidden canyon and only five had ridden out. The last one had stayed behind to ambush him. Red Dog had heard him in the rocks. He should have been more wary.

He looked back to the south. How far had he come? At least a three-hour ride, which meant the same ride back— maybe less if he let the roan gallop. But how would he transport the dead man? Tie him on the back of the stallion? That would be awkward, certainly a lot more difficult than searching the body.

Where the hell was his old partner when he needed him? Doc Weatherbee always loved going through the pockets of a dead man. To Doc, it had been like working a jigsaw puzzle or reading a newspaper. Raider didn't relish touching a dead man, unless it was to string him across his horse or bury him six feet under.

"Well," he said to the corpse. "Let's see who you are. Or who you were, boy."

But he never got to find out. As he bent down to begin his search, a rifle erupted from above, on the ridge. A big slug shattered the rock behind him, sending bits of stone flying in all directions.

Raider cried, "Shit!" and dove for the ground. He could hear the echo of the rolling breech as the rifleman above reloaded. It was probably an old buffalo gun, a Sharps or a Remington. One shot, but that might be enough.

The big man still held the reins of the roan. He leaped up, grabbing his '76 Winchester from the scabbard. Again the buffalo gun exploded, sending a slug within inches of Raider's head. He hit the ground again, wondering if his Winchester would be enough against the high-brass weapon.

The rolling breach echoed as the rifleman reloaded. It had to be Red Dog up there. How the hell was he going to get away with the buffalo gun keeping him pinned? Red Dog could just keep peppering away. He didn't even have to get closer.

Raider pulled the roan into the rocks, hoping the animal wouldn't spook again and stomp him to death.

"Hey, lawman," came the hateful cry. "Red Dog will kill you!"

Raider replied with a volley from the Winchester. Red Dog fired again, smashing the rocks above the big man's head. Raider counted the seconds as the Apache reloaded. It took him six seconds to reload the big gun.

"Kinda far from home, ain't you, Red Dog?" Raider hollered.

No reply.

"I mean, Apaches don't live up here in Montana. How come you ain't in Texas or Arizona?"

Nothing from above.

Raider looked toward the east again. It was going to be a bright morning. The clouds from the storm had faded to the south. If he was going to get away, he had better move fast.

He looked up at the roan. "I hope you're ready t' run."

The dead man was the key. Raider crawled back to him and took off his coat. Then he crawled back to the rocks and readied himself. Six seconds. It might not be enough, but it was all he had. He took a deep breath and then launched the coat into the air.

The buffalo gun exploded again.

Raider jumped into the saddle and spurred the roan out of the rocks. Counting under his breath. One-two-three. Echo of the rolling breach as Red Dog reloaded. Four-five-six. The stallion burst out of the rocks.

Raider reined hard to the left. The buffalo gun made a hellish noise. A slug whipped past the roan and slammed into the ground. Raider spurred the stallion, hoping he would be out of range in another six seconds.

Raider rode hard to the south, hoping there were no other men left to follow him. Two more shots from the big gun, but they both missed. When there was no third shot fired, Raider knew he was out of range.

As he galloped hard for the Delta Plain spread, he did not even look back at the ridge where the disappointed outlaw lay with his gun.

But the trouble did not seem to be over. Raider heard more shots as he drew closer to the Delta Plain. Then there was thunder. He reined up and gazed at the cloudless sky. The thunder kept coming.

Raider strained to look at the horizon but he could not see a thing. He had to get to higher ground. He wasn't far from the ridge that overlooked the ranch. He could make it if the stallion still had enough left after the hard ride.

"Come on, boy. One more run."

At the crest of the ridge, Raider saw the trouble below. The cattle that had been secure in their holding pens were now free and running to the east in a calamitous stampede. Men were chasing them, firing guns to keep the cattle on the run.

Raider knew what to do, but he wasn't sure he wanted to try it. The roan might be too tired to get out there and cut off the lead steer. And he might fall and be trampled to death by the cows. But the possibilities didn't mean anything unless he tried. He spurred the roan and started down the incline, driving for the mass of beef that thundered over the plain.

Oat Weeks had been dreaming of Tucson and a girl who dealt faro in a saloon there. In the dream, he had been winning at faro and at the game of love. He was all smiles until the shooting started. He looked around the saloon, trying to find the source of the gunfire. But there was no one in sight and a hand was shaking him.

"Oat. Get up."

Ease Martin was standing next to his bunk. "What the hell?"

The shots echoed from below.

As Oat climbed to his feet, he saw the other men stirring. More shots in the purple first light of dawn. Oat strapped on an old Navy Colt and followed Ease Martin onto the porch of the bunkhouse.

"Damn."

He couldn't see everything, but Oak Weeks knew that the sentries by the holding pens were no longer there. The barbed wire wasn't visible, but he figured it had been cut, otherwise how would the cattle have been able to get out? Every head that they had rounded up was running due east, some of the herd splitting Cantrell's house.

Ease Martin pulled nervously at a Remington on his hip. "There's about six of them spooking the herd. There they go, back to the south. Must've come in up the river."

Oat started for the stable. "I reckon we better give chase."

"Hold up, Oat."

He turned to look back at Ease.

"We'll never make it," Martin said. "And we're gonna have to stay here to help with the cattle."

Oat knew he was right. He glanced toward the rumbling herd. "How far you reckon they'll go?"

Martin shrugged. "Maybe two miles."

It was then that something moving down the slope caught the eyes of Oat Weeks. "Damn," he said. "It's Thornton."

Martin saw it too. He was going to ask Oat how he was sure the rider was Ray Thornton, but then he recognized the roan. Even from that distance he knew the big stallion.

"What the hell is he gonna do?" Martin asked.

Oat shook his head. "Gonna try to cut off that lead steer."

"He'll never make it."

"He's on the right pony," Oat offered.

By now the others were on the porch, watching as the roan raced toward the herd.

"Come on, big 'un!" Oat Weeks cried.

Somebody in the group said that the big rider didn't have a prayer of living, much less stopping the stampede. They all watched intently, rooting for the wild man on the roan stallion.

Raider could not believe the strength of the horse underneath him. The roan ate up the turf, driving for the lead steer like he had been born for it. Raider swung him alongside the herd, running parallel to the steers for a couple of seconds. Cows weren't very fast, not compared to the stallion.

The pounding of the hooves was deafening.

For a moment, Raider considered shooting the lead animal, but finally decided that another shot would not help matters.

So he cut in front of the cows, galloping at an angle, still outpacing the massive herd. If he stopped or fell, they'd sing songs over his grave. Or maybe a few criminals would come by to piss on his cairn.

It wasn't something he wanted to think about.

He darted ahead of the first steer, cutting to the right and easing back to run close alongside it.

"Come on, you son of a bitch!"

Raider could see the wild, red look in the animal's eye. He was a big one and still a bull, Raider saw. Had the animal not been hell-bent on running, it would have probably gored the roan with its horns.

Raider bumped the stallion into the bull, nudging it toward the left. The bull swayed a little, prompting Raider to give it another bump. Behind him, the hooves of the herd continued to roar. He had to get the bull turned north. That would force the rest of the steers to swing around, slowing them until they finally stopped.

The bull gave a bellow and swung at the roan with his horns.

Raider drove it to the left, using the body of the stallion, taking advantage of the horse's superior weight.

It seemed like forever before the bull broke free of the others, running north after Raider and his mount.

The big man easily evaded the bull's charge, turning toward the rise again. He guided the roan to the crest of the summit and looked back down at the herd. As he had hoped, the rest of the steers had slowed, swinging in a wide arc to follow the bull.

They'd be jumpy for a while, he thought, but the worst was over. He wiped the sweat from his brow. The sun was up now, the morning hot. Raider suddenly felt tired and hungry.

He had to figure out what to do. It would be risky, approaching Cantrell about Red Dog and the hidden cattle. The stampede had him confused. He knew Red Dog wasn't behind the raid, because the Apache had shot at him only hours before. Unless the Indian had planned the attack and then let his men carry out the ploy. Maybe the rival spread, Three Forks, had decided to make trouble for the Delta Plain.

It had been a damned confusing night.

Raider glanced back at the bunkhouse to see riders coming toward him. Weeks and Martin.

"Good work," Weeks said. "Nobody in this outfit woulda had the nerve to try somethin' like that."

Martin nodded. "Where'd you learn that trick?"

Raider shrugged. "I did some cowboyin' in my time. Who started this whole mess anyway?"

Weeks and Martin looked at each other and then shook their heads.

"Had to be the Three Forks boys," Martin said.

Oat was not so sure. "Coulda been Red Dog."

Raider gestured toward the herd. "You boys better get down there and help round 'em back up."

Oat Weeks smiled. "Reckon you saved ever'body a load of work."

"True enough," Ease Martin rejoined. "Them dogies would have been strewed all the way from here to Sunday."

Raider started the roan back down the slope. "I'm gonna have a look at them holdin' pens."

"Good thing I sold you that stallion!" Oat Weeks called after him.

Raider waved his Stetson and kept going toward the holding pens.

He found three sentries, all dead, with arrows in their chests. Maybe Red Dog did have something to do with the stampede. At least somebody wanted it to look that way.

The barbed wire had been snipped with cutters. An easy trick once the sentries were gone. Just open the gates, fire a few shots and you had a million tons of beef chugging across the plain.

He rode out beyond the pens to check for tracks. He picked up a fresh set heading south. The big man decided to follow them as far as he could, finding that the six riders had turned west again after a few miles.

"Now we're gettin' somewhere," he said to himself.

He patted the roan's neck. "How you doin', boy?"

The stallion snorted. A fine animal. Raider figured he'd gotten a bargain swapping the bay mare for him.

The tracks were clear and went steadily westward. Raider followed them to some high ground, where he could look back down on the Delta Plain. The men had the herd settled down now. It would probably take a couple of days to get them back into the pens.

Something else came to mind. If Cantrell's spread had been attacked, then the red-haired man might want to exact revenge on his rivals at Three Forks. The first battle of the range war had been fought. Maybe it was time to call in more help. Raider figured it was smarter to know when things were out of his hands. It might take nine or ten top agents, plus any posse that Junior Mays could raise.

He was considering procedure when he saw her. She was coming toward the Delta Plain in the surrey he had seen before. One woman alone. He strained to catch a glimpse of her. Damn, it sure looked like the woman he had known so long ago. The hair, the way she held herself.

Then something else struck him—the mistress of Three Forks was paying a call on the Delta Plain. Mac Wilson's wife was coming alone to see Cantrell. Even if it wasn't the woman he knew, he still had more than a few questions he wanted to ask her and Cantrell.

So he forgot about procedure, what he *should* do. It made

sense to find the marshal and get a telegram back to the agency, to wait until they had enough men to settle the thing once and for all. But the woman had driven those thoughts from his mind.

He made for the main house, wondering how he was going to get in without being seen.

There was no one to greet him as he rode up to the back porch. All of the men were busy with the herd. Raider stomped up the steps into the kitchen. Bright Feather looked away from the stove. Raider put a finger to his lips.

"Some doin's around here," she whispered.

Raider nodded. "Where's your boss?"

"Cantrell? He's in his den, down the hall."

Raider looked into a shadowed corridor. "I need to be where I can hear 'im without 'im seein' me."

Bright Feather giggled, suddenly glad to be involved in some sort of intrigue. She took Raider's hand and led him down the hall. At the end of the corridor, she opened a door and ushered him into a closet.

"The other side is his den," she whispered.

Raider kissed her cheek and eased in.

He could hear them talking on the other side of the door.

"You shouldn't have come here, Mrs. Wilson," Cantrell was saying. "You know as well as I do who's behind this stampede."

She told him he was wrong. Things could be settled without fighting. If he would just meet with her husband. They could talk instead of shooting.

Raider felt his breath leave him. His chest burned at the sound of her voice. It had been almost two decades, but he still knew that voice. He had to see her. He had to know for sure.

"It won't do you any good," Cantrell told her.

Raider dropped down to one knee, trying to look through the keyhole.

"Please, Mr. Cantrell, I beg you!"

Raider put his eye to the hole.

"Just leave, Mrs. Wilson. That would be the best thing. I can't be responsible for what happens if you stay here."

SINS OF THE GUNSLINGER 101

She moved into his range of vision. Raider felt his stomach coming to life, flip-flopping like he had swallowed a live trout. It was her. After all those years of thinking he would never see her again.

He had to say her name. "Thalia."

A finger tapped him on the shoulder.

He reached back, trying to shoo Bright Feather away.

A revolver cylinder clicked and he felt cold iron on his neck.

"Don't move, partner," said Johnny Dallas.

Raider froze, still stunned from seeing the woman.

"On your feet," Dallas said. "Raise them hands, too."

Raider obeyed. Dallas removed Raider's Colt from its holster. Raider just stood there, almost unable to move.

"Mr. Cantrell's gonna want to know why you were spyin' on him," the gunslinger said. "He ain't gonna like it."

But for some reason, Raider didn't give two hoots in hell what Cantrell liked or didn't like. It was the woman, Thalia, suddenly appearing here in the middle of all this trouble. One of those stray bullets that life sent you, the kind that got you in the heart.

CHAPTER ELEVEN

Dallas led him back to the kitchen, where Raider waited at gunpoint. The slick gunslinger was careful. He made sure Raider was tied hand and foot and then put him in a chair with a rope around his chest. The big Pinkerton did not resist, but sat there thinking how much the sight of one woman could weaken him to the point of no resistance. In his daze, he never stopped to consider the effects of a whole night in the saddle.

Bright Feather tried to bring him coffee.

"Get back," Dallas said, waving her away with the Colt.

Raider's eyes narrowed. "There's no need to talk to her like that."

"Squaws are bad luck," the shootist insisted. "Hell, look at all that's happened since you brought them here."

"That stampede ain't no fault o' theirs," Raider replied.

Dallas focused his weasely gaze on the big man from Arkansas. "Well maybe you know exactly who's fault it was."

Raider didn't take the bait. He knew he would be facing Cantrell soon enough. No need to argue with the hired hand.

The gunslinger turned back to watch as Cantrell ushered the woman out of the house. Raider could not see her from where he was sitting, but he could still hear her voice. It was no one else but her, Thalia Anderson, somewhat older, but every bit as beautiful as she had been eighteen years ago.

When the surrey rattled off to the west, Raider strained to look out the window, just for one more glimpse of her.

But she was gone, heading back to her husband.

Raider no longer thought about solving the mystery of Red Dog, nor did he consider the facts at hand. He only wondered how he was going to get Thalia away from the danger. If she was hurt . . . he stopped himself. How could he be thinking like that? Was there still a fire burning somewhere in his heart? He had to steady himself, get his head back.

"Come on, big 'un."

Dallas untied the chest rope and led Raider through the main parlor of the house. The dapper gunman held a safe distance, keeping his piece trained on the man who had whipped big Lockett. No need to take chances with one as mean as the black-eyed intruder.

Asa Cantrell was sitting behind a desk that had belonged to the former owner of the ranch. He looked out of place, shifting nervously. Raider expected more hostility from the man, but Cantrell only seemed worried.

The red-haired man came right to the point. "You start that stampede, Thornton?"

Raider exhaled and shook his head. "No. I stopped it. Get your boys, Weeks and Martin. They'll tell you."

Johnny Dallas was standing behind Raider. Cantrell told him to go get Weeks and Martin. Told him to hurry.

When the gunfighter had gone, Cantrell hefted a huge Remington .44, sitting on his desk. "Just in case you get any ideas," he warned Raider.

The big man chortled. "Used to carry a Remington."

Cantrell did not seem to hear him.

"Lost it in a river an' started carryin' my Peacemaker. Like the feel o' the forty-five. Lot easier to find shells for it, too."

Cantrell's sun-weary face wrinkled in an accusatory expression. "Why was you in that closet listenin' like a sneak?"

"The woman," Raider replied. "I had to see her."

That was partially true.

"Then you know Mrs. Wilson?"

Raider looked sadly at the floor. "I did. A while back."

Cantrell touched the butt of the Remington. "I knew you was workin' for Wilson. Knew it the minute I set eyes on you."

"No." His voice was defeated. "I ain't workin' for Wilson. I never met the man."

The red-haired man pointed a finger at him. "Then why did you stampede my cattle?"

Before Raider could offer any defense, Dallas returned with Weeks and Martin. Both of them seemed to be unsure why they were there. Oat Weeks frowned when he saw Raider's hands were tied.

Cantrell pointed at the big man. "This one says he stopped the stampede. Says you saw it."

Oat Weeks nodded. "Sure as sugar, Mr. Cantrell. Rode that roan of mine—leastways it used to be mine—cut off that lead bull like he was breakin' a wean calf from its mother."

Martin was quick to join in. "Yes sir, Mr. Cantrell. You ain't never seen nothin' like it. Thornton here rode down that ridge like he was on flat ground. Bore right in front of the herd."

Cantrell seemed puzzled by their testimonies. He looked at Raider and then back at his two men. Raider knew what Cantrell was thinking: maybe they were all working together.

"Shoulda put on more men at the pens," Weeks offered.

Cantrell replied that when Oat Weeks got his own ranch, he could decide how many men to put out on guard duty. With that, he dismissed both men and looked back at Raider. Dallas was behind the big man, holding his Colt.

"Why'd you cut off the stampede?" Cantrell asked.

Raider shrugged. "I just did. Course, I wouldn'ta done it if I'da knowed you was gonna tie me up."

Cantrell stood up but then sat back down. "What else you know about that stampede, Thornton? Come clean with me."

Raider sat up a little straighter. "All I know is what I saw when I rode down to th' holdin' pens."

"And what was that?"

"Six men," Raider replied. "Rode up from the south, or at least that was the way they wanted it t' look. After they killed the sentries with Indian arrows . . ."

Cantrell scowled at him. "Arrows?"

"That's what I said."

"Then Red Dog was behind it!" Dallas said.

Raider shook his head. "Maybe not. I had words with Red Dog earlier this mornin'. North o' here. One o' his men jumped me and we had it out. I killed the man and then exchanged shots with the Apache, only he had me outgunned from the git go. I managed to leave 'im while he was reloadin'. Then I came back here an' saw the stampede. You know the rest."

Cantrell leaned back, seemingly befuddled. "You say that my men were killed with arrows, but Red Dog didn't do it!"

"Not personally. Maybe some o' his men did. Then again, maybe you know who his men are."

Cantrell took exception to this. "I don't care what Wilson says, I ain't workin' with Red Dog. Hell, why would I stampede my own cattle? Why would I rustle from myself?"

Raider shrugged. "A reason a man does somethin' ain't always clear at first. Sometimes he tries to make somethin' look one way when it's really another. That's a good way t' start trouble an' keep it goin'."

"I ain't the one startin' the trouble," Cantrell insisted.

"I heard the woman say her husband wanted t' talk it out."

Cantrell's face turned red. "She may be a good woman, for all I know. I have to say she has guts, comin' here after her husband's men started my cows runnin' wild. But it ain't her who's in charge of Three Forks. Her husband calls the shots."

Raider leaned forward a little. "Red Dog could be the one behind all of it, Cantrell. I know he's out there. I seen 'im. I know what he's up to."

"You say the riders that stampeded my cows turned west?" Raider nodded.

"West for Three Forks," Cantrell said.

"Maybe," Raider replied, "but I'm tellin' you, somebody is settin' this up like they want it to look a certain way. But we can't tell if that's the truth. Not yet. There's a core in every apple. You get my meanin'?"

Cantrell was still skeptical. "You say Red Dog is an Apache."

"I know an Apache when I see one."

Dallas scoffed. "Ever'body knows that Red Dog is a Cheyenne half-breed."

Raider kept his temper, glaring at the shootist. "It don't make a lot o' sense, but it's true. An' Red Dog wouldn't be the first renegade to come north. Ever hear of Tal?"

"Comanche, wasn't he?" Dallas asked.

Raider nodded. "Rode all the way t' Wyomin' lookin' for trouble."

"And you say he's north of here?" Cantrell asked, full of doubt.

"He is."

"What's he doin'?"

Raider leaned back, shifting in his chair. "Now that's where this gets tricky. If I tell you, and you are workin' with Red Dog, it don't matter 'cause you already know. And if you ain't workin' with Red Dog, then knowin' where he's at might make you do somethin' stupid."

Cantrell scoffed again. "You sayin' one renegade could bring down my whole crew?"

"He's got help," Raider replied. "I know, I killed one o' them this mornin'. Or at least that stallion did."

Cantrell got up, pacing back and forth. He looked at Dallas, who nodded. The red-haired man glared at Raider. Cantrell was about to show his hole card.

"There's been some talk of a Pinkerton in these parts," he said coldly. "Said the territorial governor called him in to make sure things didn't get out of hand between me and Wilson."

Raider smiled, able to conceal his true feelings after years of working with disguises. "Well, if I see any Pinkerton, I'll be sure to shoot 'im for you, Mr. Cantrell."

Dallas cocked his Colt and pressed the bore into Raider's ear. "Don't get funny, Thornton. We know who you are. One of our scouts ran into old Tinker at his store. Said he was complainin' because the Pinkerton stole both his squaws. Described a man looked just like you. Black eyes and all."

Raider laughed. "You ever know a man t' lose a woman and not blame somebody else? Besides, Cantrell here took those squaws and I'm pretty sure he ain't no Pinkerton."

Cantrell squinted at the big man. "You're the Pinkerton, aren't you? Just fess up and I'll let you go."

"If you ain't doin' nothin' wrong, then it don't matter if I'm a Pinkerton or not," Raider challenged. "If you got nothin' t' hide, then it don't matter who knows your business, does it?"

Cantrell sighed. "Lock him in the basement, Dallas. Until I decide what to do with him."

He started to pull Raider to his feet but the big man shrugged him off. "The woman," he said.

Cantrell frowned. "What about her?"

"She's married to Mac Wilson?"

Cantrell nodded. "They got a boy, about sixteen years old. I hear tell that he's as ornery as his daddy."

Raider had to steady himself to keep his voice from cracking. "When I knew her, she was a good woman. I find it hard to believe that she would marry a man who would be mixed up in this kind o' trouble."

"Wilson is a back-shooter!" Cantrell insisted. "I don't care if his little wife is teachin' Sunday school eight days a week. I bought this spread and come here fair and squarelike. Now correct me if I'm wrong, but last I heard, this is a free country."

"But why would Wilson want you gone?" Raider asked. "There's plenty o' damned land here. Enough for ten ranches, much less two."

Cantrell slammed his fist into the desk. "Damn it, I don't know! I just know I'm gonna get even before it's through. Do you hear me?"

Raider heard him. He stood up and started to walk out in front of the gunslinger. A word from Cantrell stopped them.

Raider turned back to look at the rancher.

"For stoppin' the herd," Cantrell said, "I mean, well . . . just thanks. That's all."

Raider glared at him. "If you don't turn me loose, you ain't gonna have a hell of a lot t' be thankful for. Just remember that I said it."

"Lock him in the basement," Cantrell commanded. "And don't untie his hands or his feet."

"Yes sir, Mr. Cantrell. Whatever you say."

Raider expected the cellar to be a dank and rotten hole that smelled like buffalo shit.

Instead, the small enclosure was a rock-walled room with a mattress and a supply of candles. There was even a window that was open enough for fresh air to flow through. Raider wondered if he might be able to widen the window enough to crawl through it, but he decided that the ropes on his hands and feet were going to slow him down some.

Raider reclined on the mattress, rustling on the cornhusks. He worked for a while on the knots of the ropes, but Dallas had been smart enough to wet the cord, making it almost impossible to untie them, so he leaned back and tried to think about the situation.

He wondered if maybe he should have told Cantrell about Red Dog's hidden cattle. Then he considered the tracks that had led west away from the empty holding pens, back toward Three Forks. Maybe Cantrell was right. Maybe the men from Three Forks had started the stampede. Then again, if Cantrell wanted to keep the fight going, he could have faked the evidence to make it look like the Three Forks crew had spooked his herd.

One thing for sure: Red Dog was alive and stealing cattle. Maybe both sides were pointing the finger, using the renegade Apache as an excuse to mix it up. But why the hell did they have to fight? There was enough land, water, and buffalo grass to feed every cow in the territory. Unless there was something Raider had missed, he couldn't see the need for a skirmish. It just didn't make sense.

After a while, he wearied of thinking and closed his eyes.

She was there again. Thalia Anderson. She looked up at him, her coral lips parting slightly. He bent to kiss her, his first love, and the only one who had ever gotten to him. But there was no expectation in her lips, no words of marriage. So he kissed her.

They walked for a while, through a meadow back in Cheyenne. Raider had been trying to sign on as an army scout at Ft. Laramie but a colonel had told him he was too young to scout. Thalia put her hand on his cheek and said not to worry. Maybe he could find a job in Cheyenne.

So he tried bartending, just to be with her. That soft, white skin, her blue eyes, thick head of hair. It wasn't just the way she looked either, although she had been uncommonly beautiful. She had a way of talking; she could convince a man he could do anything if he sat and listened to her long enough.

The northlands were starting to be settled more, Thalia told him. With patience and a few good breeding animals he could build up a herd of cows and horses in no time. Land and livestock made you rich, she said. She even helped him to open a savings account at Wyoming's first bank. Her father would give her the rest of her dowry when they were married.

They could settle any piece of land that Raider liked. After all, he was going to be the gentleman rancher.

And he had actually believed it. They even started to share the things that man and wife enjoyed—including a bed. He was hesitant at first, but she told him it was all right, as long as they went through with the ceremony.

Raider had wanted to join her at the altar. But something happened inside him. At her urging, he had ridden south to look at some horses, two sorrel mares and a big black stallion. He saw the animals and decided not to buy them. He had saddled up again and looked to the north.

He could not get started. He knew what lay back in Cheyenne. If he returned, she would have him forever. Twenty years old and stuck in the mud. He hadn't even seen California.

He rode west instead of north.

But there she was, back in his arms, telling him it was all right after all those years. She had understood. Now she would get rid of her husband and Raider could quit the service.

Their lips pressed together.

He told her he would love her forever, that he always had.

She spoke his name.

"Raider!"

Suddenly her face had changed and she had begun to poke him hard in the shoulder.

"Raider, open your eyes."

The voice was different.

He sat up on the mattress, soaked with sweat.

Bright Feather was looking at him. Her hands were on his face. He caught his breath, forgetting his dream in an instant.

Bright Feather frowned at him. "You were dreaming about that woman, weren't you?"

Raider remembered he was the captive of Asa Cantrell. "How the hell did you get down here?" he asked the girl.

Bright Feather shrugged. "I brought you something."

She started to lift her dress, laughing playfully before she dropped it.

"A man hates a tease," Raider grumbled.

She giggled and offered him a tray of food: cold beans, potatoes, some beef, and a few wild onions.

Raider didn't waste any time devouring all of it.

She had some kind of brew also, a homeade ale. Raider drank it slow, wondering if it had been drugged. The drink rang his head a little.

"We can't do it if you're tied up like that," said Bright Feather.

Raider grunted. "Ain't in the mood. You hear anything up there? Anything about me or what they're gonna do t' me?"

Her wide eyes dropped. "They asked me if you're a Pinkerton."

He grabbed her shoulders. "What did you say?"

"I told them you were."

He fought the urge to slap her. Then he finally decided it didn't matter. They knew, even if he wasn't admitting it, that he was a Pink.

"I reckon they'll bury me deep," he said sadly. "Shit, I didn't do anybody any good on this one."

She slid next to him, putting her hand on his thigh. "You did me good, cowboy. You can do it again."

He brushed her hand away. "Leave me alone, Bright Feather."

The girl continued rubbing his chest. "Where you're going there probably won't be any loving," she offered.

That made more sense than he cared to admit.

"I mean, why wouldn't you want to do it one more time before they hang you?" Bright Feather said. "I'd be happy to be your last pleasure on this earth. It could be nice."

He let her hand wander over to his crotch. She rubbed him through the cloth for a while before she started on the buttons. Raider grabbed her wrist. She frowned and tried to pull away.

Raider held her fast, kissing her on the forehead. The kiss toned her down some. She relaxed, pressing against him.

"I like you," she said. "I really do. You're a good man, Ray."

"And you're a good woman," he replied. "I just want t' take it my way this time. It is my last request after all."

She nodded, saying she would do whatever he said.

Raider asked her to cut his bonds. She did so without hesitation, using a kitchen knife that she had hidden in the folds of her calico dress. Raider rubbed his wrists, thinking he would keep the knife and maybe dig out later. He could try widening the small window. That would have to wait, however. At the moment, Raider's senses were completely enraptured by the Indian girl. He smelled her hair and her skin, fresh from a lilac bath. And he knew her to be receptive in every way to his advances. That, and his close proximity to death, heightened his desires.

He found himself wanting to do things he had not tried in years.

"Let's get our clothes off," he said.

They stripped bare and Bright Feather pressed her brown body into his. Raider kissed her for a moment, lowering his lips to the tight circles of her dark nipples. Her hand gripped his prick, pulling at it.

"I want it in me," she whispered.

"Not yet."

The girl looked up at him, wondering what the man with black eyes had in mind. he told her to lie down on the mattress. Spread her legs. Close her eyes. Just wait for him.

"What are you going to do?" she asked.

Raider knelt at her feet. "I'm going to kiss your pussy," he replied. "Don't ask me why, I just feel like doin' it."

She grabbed his head and pulled him between her thighs.

Raider mouthed the pink folds of her cunt until her body stiffened and started to quiver. He tried to come up for air but she wouldn't let him. He stayed between her legs for a long time, driving her to one shivering orgasm after another.

Finally he could not stand it any longer. "Woman, are you gonna let me get mine, or what?"

She looked up at him through half-slitted, dreamy eyes. "No man ever done that to me before."

"Well, I don't expect any man ever will again," Raider replied. "That's a trick you only see in the finer whorehouses west of the Mississippi."

He was not ashamed to talk about his whoring. He didn't expect that would go over too well with St. Peter, but now he felt like sharing his knowledge with the girl. His mind recalled everything he had ever done with a chippy. He was going to do it all to her, he thought.

But naturally, Bright Feather, being of the female persuasion, was apt to surprises at any time. "I want to do it to you," she said. "You put your mouth on me, now I want to put my mouth on you."

He considered refusing, but then he realized that he found the idea agreeable. She did it to him, although she wasn't very good at it. He told her she was, though, and she managed to excite him to the point where he could not restrain himself any longer. He made her lie down on her back.

Bright Feather seemed to be in another world. Her eyes rolled back when he penetrated her. She didn't cry out or whimper, but her body began to move in perfect rhythm with his.

She wanted it every way he could give it to her: on top, from behind, legs on shoulders, sideways, her on top, from behind again. Raider finally came, collapsing on top of her.

They lay on the mattress, trying to catch their breaths.

The air was cool, tingling their sweaty bodies.

Bright Feather nestled into his chest. "I'm sorry I told them you were a Pinkerton."

"I reckon they knew anyway."

She hesitated, twirling her fingers in his chest hair. "Ray..."

"Huh?"

"Ray, they're planning something upstairs. I know it. I heard them talking about Red Dog."

Raider sat up. "What'd they say?"

"I don't know exactly. But they were talking about you, too. I think they're afraid to believe you."

"I need to know exactly what they said," he urged her. "Can you remember anything at all?"

She shook her head. She couldn't remember any more of the conversation than what she'd already told him. She was sorry. She wanted to repay him somehow. He told her the meal was enough. He stretched out again on the mattress.

"What time is it?" he asked her.

"It was six when I came down," she replied.

Raider glanced up at the small window to see the shadows

darkening outside. Good. He needed it to be dark. He'd wait a while, until things settled down. Then he'd try to dig out that window. If he could escape and get to the stable, he might have a chance to outrun them. His roan would be rested and ready to go again.

"Ray, I want to repay you," the girl said.

Her hand went down to his prick. Her mouth followed. She was better the second time and Raider regained his erection. The second time was less arduous, but more tender. She told him to take it slow when he entered, because she was sore.

But she seemed to forget the soreness in a hurry, quickening her motion, bucking Raider to his second release.

When they were finished, she offered to stay the night. Raider told her just to go back upstairs, to tell Cantrell that he was resting peacefully with no thoughts of escape. She agreed to do what he said, kissed him good-bye, and left with the empty tray. He had to call her back to remind her put on her dress. She apologized, saying that she was sad about his situation.

"You and me both, lady."

When she was gone, he decided to rest awhile, to listen, to formulate some sort of plan.

But he quickly fell asleep again, this time without dreams.

When he opened his eyes three hours later, he had to rub them to make sure he was not lost in some dreamscape.

Things had changed while he had been unconscious.

And he could not decide if he should take the bait.

CHAPTER TWELVE

Raider saw his Colt sitting in front of him on the floor. His '76 Winchester was there too. Both of them had been shined and oiled. It had to be a dream.

He reached out and grabbed the redwood handle of the Peacemaker.

"Yeah!"

It felt good in his hand. He spun the cylinder, which was tight and smooth. He expected both weapons to be empty—a cruel trick played by Cantrell. That was the gambit. Give him weapons without ammunition and let him try to leave. They'd shoot him down in a second.

But the Colt was fully loaded, all six cylinders. There were cartridges in the Winchester too. Maybe the guns had been rigged to explode.

Cantrell was one crazy son of a bitch. Leaving him loaded iron. Maybe the bullets were dummies. No way to fire and check it out. They'd hear him.

Looking at his guns, Raider figured Cantrell would expect him to go out the front door. Just sashay up the steps and try to shoot his way to a mount. Raider didn't want to disappoint Cantrell; he planned to leave all right. Only he was going to use the kitchen knife to dig out the window casement and make the opening big enough for him to climb through.

It didn't take long to dig out the casement. Some dirt and mortar fell back on him, but that only helped to make the escape hole bigger. He listened, expecting someone to stick a gun in his face. But there didn't seem to be much movement around the Delta Plain. Maybe Cantrell had most of his men riding night herd.

He lifted the guns again to look at them. He hoped he

wasn't dreaming. He didn't want to wake up on the cornhusk mattress with his cock in his hand and a rope around his neck.

"Here goes nothin'."

After pushing the guns out into the yard, he started through the hole himself. The fit was tight. He thought for a moment that he might have to squeeze back down and do some more digging. But at last his torso broke free and he crawled out into the dusty night.

As he rose to his feet, he heard the click of a pistol.

"I told them you wouldn't go through the cellar door," said the gunfighter, Johnny Dallas. "You're not the type to do what's expected of you."

Behind Dallas stood Raider's stallion. The big roan had a wild look in its eye, like it knew death was coming. His guns lay at his feet on the ground, collecting dust as he would soon be doing.

"Just gonna shoot me and lay me over my horse?" he asked. "Then the marshal will find me and y'all can say Red Dog done it."

The gunslinger's countenance slacked into a vague expression of approval. "You know, Ray, you think a lot like a criminal. Did anyone ever tell you that?"

Raider shrugged. "Comes with the terr'tory. You ever killed a Pinkerton before, Dallas?"

The shootist shook his head. "Can't say I have. Maybe killed one by accident and didn't know it."

The wall was behind him. He could drop for one of the guns, roll, try to get off a lucky shot. No way to go right or left. Dallas would be too quick. Besides, he was already drawn.

"Ever kiss my ass, Dallas?"

A sad frown from the hired gun. "No need to get rude. I ain't done nothin' to you, Ray."

The drop would be the best move. Hell, Dallas was going to get him. He'd have to take a slug. Maybe it would kill him. Maybe not.

"Don't go for the Colt, Ray. You're fast, but I'd get you."

Raider measured the distance to the gunman. If he could leap, take a round, get his hands on the bastard's throat, he could take Dallas with him.

But the dapper gunman didn't pull the trigger. He simply stepped aside and handed the reins of the roan to Raider. The big man hesitated. Did the outlaw want to shoot him off the horse?

"You ain't good enough to hit me at a run," Raider said.

Dallas motioned with the barrel of his Colt. "Just stand over by the stallion. Go on, do like I say."

Raider slid over next to the roan. Dallas told him to climb in the saddle. Raider obeyed, wondering if he could get the stallion to rear and stomp Dallas into the ground. But as soon as he mounted, Dallas picked up the Colt and the '76 Winchester and came toward him.

Dallas hung Raider's gunbelt over the saddle horn and then dropped the '76 into the rifle scabbard.

Raider wanted to pinch himself. This couldn't be happening. He was going to wake up next to Bright Feather.

He peered down at the smirking face of Johnny Dallas. "What's goin' on round here, honcho?"

Dallas dropped his Colt into his holster. He patted the roan on the neck. "Just go, big man. Do what you have to do. And when the chips are down and the truth flying over your head, just remember who helped you."

"I got you t' thank for this?"

"Thank the Delta Plain Cattle Company, pardner. Hyah!"

Dallas gave the stallion a slap and it ran north into the night.

Raider no longer expected to wake up in bed. He had some things running around in his head, reasons for what had happened. He'd sort it out later, when he had played another hand with Red Dog.

As he galloped over the spring turf, he saw the lights of the bunkhouse above on the rise. He felt like taking a chance. If he was wrong, it might mean drawing his Colt. But if he was right, it could make things a whole lot easier—and clearer—down the road.

The roan mounted the slope with ease. Raider reined back in front of the bunkhouse. It wasn't late enough for anyone to be asleep.

"Weeks!" he called at the top of his voice. "Martin! Roll your butts out here right now."

He didn't have to call again. Oat Weeks and Ease Martin came running out of the bunkhouse. The other hands were too afraid to face Raider, so they hung back, watching from the windows.

"Whatchoo want, Ray?" Oat Weeks asked cautiously.

"Yeah," echoed Ease Martin. "Whatchoo want?"

Raider glared down at them, hoping he had not made a mistake. Their hands were hanging over their pistols. He had never seen them draw so he was not sure if he could get both of them in one pop.

He decided to blurt it out. "Weeks, you and Ease seem like the only boys in this outfit that can tell your asses from a hole in the ground."

That sat just right with Weeks, who straightened proudly.

Martin wasn't so sure. "They say you're a Pinkerton, Ray. Say you come here to hurt Mr. Cantrell."

"I ain't come t' hurt nobody. I come t' help. Now I know where Red Dog is and I need a couple o' men t' help me smoke 'im out. If y'all ain't up t' the job, just wave me off and I'll go try t' get 'im myself. I never figured either o' you t' be the kind t' slack on a task."

Martin looked at Oat. "He wants us to ride with him. A Pinkerton."

"What about our jobs here?" Oat asked.

Raider exhaled impatiently. "Not that it matters, but I can guarantee you day wages as an operative o' the Pinkerton agency. Whatever you're gettin' here, I can pay it."

Oat nodded appreciatively. "I'm game."

Ease still wasn't so sure. "Red Dog is dangerous, Oat. I don't know if the three of us should tangle with him."

Raider turned the stallion north again. "I'm goin'. If y'all want t' ride with me, meet me at the beginnin' o' that long ridge. You know what I'm talkin' 'bout?"

Oat said he did and that he would be there. Raider spurred to the north with the realization that Oat was going to have to do some more talking to his partner. Raider figured it didn't matter. All he really wanted to do was some scouting. Even if Weeks and Martin did come along, he was only going to send them to the nearest town for a message back to the agency as soon as the scouting was over.

The moon was rising as he drove toward the ridge. He stopped on another rise, gazing west toward Three Forks. His heart started to beat rapidly. Was it thoughts of the woman? Or something else, something that he was starting to see, something that he hoped wasn't true. Maybe it would all work out after he got it straight.

Ease Martin didn't feel right about riding out into the night, but he did it anyway. Oat was the leader of the pair, the head partner. Ease usually deferred to Oat, even if the stocky cowboy did have a dangerous sense of adventure. Ease had been figuring to break with Oat as soon as they drew their wages from Cantrell. But now he was following his partner after some crazy Pinkerton.

Oat rode ahead of him on Raider's old mare, watching the ridge.

Weeks trailed him on a mule. "Are you sure this is where he told us to meet him?"

Oat replied, "Yeah, that's what he said."

"I can't say I like this, Oat. We was better off when we was back with Cantrell. Now we ain't even got jobs."

Oat chortled disgustedly. "You can't see your face because your nose is in the way. We're gonna be Pinkertons, Ease. All we have to do is come through for this fella and he'll tell his agency to hire us."

A rifle lever chortled. "Not necessarily."

Raider dropped down in front of them from a rock.

Oat Weeks reined the mare. "Damn, where'd you come from?"

Ease Martin stopped the mule. "That weren't funny, Ray. You scared me half to death."

Raider started walking back into the shadows of the rocks. "Anybody can't take it, clear out now. We got a long night ahead of us."

"Hear that?" Oat Weeks said excitedly. "A long night."

Raider came back leading the roan. "I heard you two comin' for an hour before you got here. You gotta be quiet."

"We can be quiet," Weeks assured him. "Can't we, Ease."

"Yeah, I reckon," Martin replied dolefully.

"Then shut up! We still got a couple hours o' ridin' ahead

of us. Y'all stay back about two hundred feet. If I get shot, turn tail an' ride back t' Delta Plain. Tell Cantrell an' Dallas what happened."

Oat nodded dutifully, watching as Raider loped north on the stallion.

They fell in behind him, staying back as he had ordered.

Ease Martin didn't like the moon as it rose. He didn't care for the terrain, or his mule. In fact, he didn't like the feel of the whole damned night. He wanted to say something to Oat about it, but he remembered that the Pinkerton had warned them to keep quiet. So he just held the mule steady, eating dust from the stallion's pounding hooves.

Raider crouched low in the shadows, moving slowly like a gila monster in a north Texas snowstorm. He was stripped to the waist, dark smudges all over his body, rubbed with dirt so the sweat wouldn't sparkle in the rays of the moon. He had been stalking for the better part of two hours, carefully working his way back to the hidden herd.

Weeks and Martin were stationed in some boulders about a half mile back, with orders to run for help if they heard any shooting, or if Raider wasn't back by morning. As he pulled himself over a rock, he wondered if they could be trusted. It had been a gamble to bring them along, but better than rolling the dice against Red Dog without any backup at all. Though he also couldn't help but feel that two yokels from Montana might not come up to Wagner's standards for agency operatives.

A breeze came up, bringing the smell of the cattle to Raider. He stopped, assessing the direction of the odor. He was close. But that might mean Red Dog was also nearby.

He kept on, making for the box canyon.

His approach was from the southeast, a different angle than his first trip. He didn't dare walk along the regular path. Not after he had sent Red Dog's man to perdition.

He found a narrow path between the rocks. It led him up to the rim of the box canyon. The animals were below, although they had no blue fire on their horns this night. Only the light of moon glinted off them.

No sounds of Red Dog. Raider checked his Colt and his

knife, both of which were in his right boot. His heart was thumping. He considered the idea of looking for Red Dog in the night. A *mano y mano* Injun fight in the dark. It could be a way to settle everything. Bringing in the body of Red Dog might put an end to the range war.

He lowered his legs down the side and started to feel his way into the canyon. Slow meant quiet. Raider hardly breathed as he descended. He remembered the way Red Dog had turned and looked at him that dark morning. He had made little more noise than a cactus growing, but the Apache had leered straight at him.

Apaches were tough and keen, he had to give them that. They were as mean as a Blackfoot and as crazy as a Comanche. Savage too, although Comanches were usually considered to be the coarsest heathens west of the Mississippi. Given a choice, Raider would have rather chased an Apache through the dark. Comanches gave him nightmares.

He reached the bottom of the canyon without any trouble. No one shot at him or jumped him. But as soon as he turned to face the cows, he felt stupid. There he stood with several hundred head of cattle ready to stomp right over him.

Working his way along the canyon wall, he managed to avoid the animals' horns, eventually coming to a crude wooden gate that blocked the exit path. Suddenly he had a brilliant idea. He'd coax the lead steer out onto the path and the cattle would follow him back onto the plain. They'd smell the water from the south and naturally head that way. He could pick up Weeks and Martin and drive the cows back to the Delta Plain. Or somewhere. He'd tell somebody about Red Dog's hidden herd.

It took him a while to get one of the steers through the gate, but after he got the animal rolling, the others fell right into line. Raider emerged from the path, running south again to find his partners.

"Weeks, Martin. Head 'em up. We gotta hurry. Get your mounts."

Raider ran toward the spot where he had left them, but he did not hear them or see them now.

Rushing around in the rocks, he turned into a nook where he had left the roan. The animal was still there. Where were the other two mounts? Had the Montana tinhorns mounted up and headed for home? Raider couldn't have blamed them if they had.

As he was leading the roan out toward the plain, he tripped over something on the ground. He knew it was a body. There was another one lying right next to it. Oat Weeks and his partner. He took a closer look and saw that their throats had been cut.

"Red Dog. That bastard."

He started to swing into the saddle of the roan. But suddenly there were ropes in the air, two lassos that dropped over him and tightened. Someone pulled him off the roan. He went for his gun as he fell. But he never got the Colt out of the holster.

A hard object hit him in the back of the head.

His eyes seemed to lose focus.

"Red Dog," he muttered.

Something struck him again.

The next thing he knew, it was really hot, the sun beating down all around him.

He had been out for a while.

He tried to sit up, but he couldn't.

The sun was blinding.

A shadow came between him and the sun. He saw the Apache standing over him. Red Dog smelled as bad as the cattle.

"I killed your friends," the Apache said with a cheerful leer. "It was pretty easy. I waited until you started climbing down into the canyon."

Raider's mouth was dry. "Why didn't you just kill me then?"

Red Dog laughed. His face was as sun dried as an adobe house. Raider tried to see if the Indian had others with him, but found that he could not even turn his head. He was staked down with rawhide, his arms and legs spread eagle, lashed to heavy wooden stobs. His head had been fixed as well, not to mention the wet rawhide around his neck.

Red Dog touched Raider's bonds. "Wet rawhide shrinks down fast," he said. "Many think Apaches invented this trick.

But my father told me it was invented by a white man."

"I know the trick," Raider said.

Red Dog smiled appreciatively. "I thought you would know it. But I will tell it anyway."

Raider figured he was a damned mean-looking Apache. But then, with his body staked to the ground, he figured to be a mite prejudiced. Why had he gone back to the ridge? To face Red Dog, he told himself.

Now he was facing him, looking up.

Red Dog touched the rawhide strip at his neck. "It dries out and then shrinks," the Indian said. "It cuts into your wrists and ankles. Also your head and neck. Now sometimes, it doesn't shrink far enough. So you don't die of strangling. You die slower."

"You're a true comfort to the weary, Red Dog."

He felt the sun all around him. Even if the shrinking rawhide didn't kill him, he wouldn't last long in the sun. It would bake his brains and make him crazy. Then the scavengers would eat him alive. He had heard stories of coyotes digging into a live man, but he had never believed it.

Red Dog eyed the rawhide strips. "The thing is, will you strangle or will you just die from the heat?"

"I'd bet on either one."

It was hard to talk. His tongue was getting bigger. This was a horrible way to die. But he planned to make the best of it.

"I usually like to strap a man to an anthill," Red Dog went on. "A Mexican anthill if I can find it."

"Cover a man with honey, so the ants will get 'im?" Raider offered.

A shrug from the Apache. "I never used honey. I just opened some cuts and let a little blood flow. Ants like blood better than honey."

"I hope I can use that knowledge someday."

Red Dog frowned. "You know, there's not one decent anthill in Montana. I don't even know why I came up here."

"Every terr'tory has its drawbacks," Raider conceded.

Red Dog nodded. "True enough. Well, I better leave you to die."

The shadow left Raider's face, relinquishing his body to the sun.

"Red Dog!"

The Indian turned back to look at him. "Last words, white man?"

Raider tried to spit but he didn't have anything but cotton in his mouth. "When my death is learned of by my boss, you'll have a hundred Pinks crawling all over your ass. They'll hang you from the highest tree."

Red Dog made a sweeping gesture. "I don't see a tree for miles. I guess they'll have to drag me all the way to the mountains."

Raider couldn't see them, but he heard four horses riding away. "Damn, that's one difficult Injun."

He could feel the rawhide starting to shrink. The sun wasn't going to give him a break. He wondered if he would choke first or if he would die from the brutal heat.

The leather was tight around his throat when the clouds blew in. Raider prayed for the rain. He figured it might buy him a few minutes. At least the sun had gone behind the clouds.

He could barely breathe when the deluge broke. The water loosened the rawhide, but not enough for him to get free. At least the air didn't wheeze as it went down his throat.

Another fear gripped him as the rain fell. He wondered if he might drown in a puddle. The water seemed to run off for a while, but then it started to gather. Before he could worry more about it, the rain stopped and the sun came back out again.

The rawhide strips were so wet that they didn't tighten much until afternoon. By then, most of the water was gone from around him. He prayed for rain again, thinking it would be better to drown than to strangle.

But the rawhide didn't cut off his wind, and another storm at dusk loosened up his bonds again.

He tried to get leverage on his stakes, to pull them out of the wet ground. Red Dog had driven the stobs in deep. It might take a good strong mule to pull them out.

That Indian had lassoed him right out of the saddle. Or had he? He didn't recall seeing Red Dog handling a rope.

He shook himself from the inside. His thoughts were becoming looser. The rain had gotten him through the day, but the sun would come again. He could do little more than lie there and wait to die.

After dark, he managed to go to sleep for a while. He woke up once in the night to see a coyote standing over him. Raider shouted and the animal ran away. After that he stayed awake until the rain came again.

All he had to do was open his mouth and let the water fall in. He would have it made if the rain kept up. Just lie there until someone found him.

Of course, Red Dog would be back to check on him, especially with all the rain. But he wouldn't come back for a while. That left open the possibility that someone would happen along and free him.

But the rain disappeared and the sun came out again.

By noon, Raider was turning blue from the tight rawhide around his neck. He could still breathe, but only enough to keep from dying outright. His head had left him too. He was floating on a cloud and there were lot of people around him.

He knew them all, friends and enemies from his past. He began to talk to them, finishing conversations, shaking hands. It went on all day, even after a shower loosened the rawhide. Delerium had set in and it stayed right through the night.

When he wasn't sleeping, he was raving. He cursed everyone from his past who had betrayed him. Then he told them all he was sorry.

He talked to Thalia again. And to Wagner. Then his former partner, Doc Weatherbee. In the hallucination, Doc was bouncing a towheaded baby on his knee. He cursed Doc, telling him none of this would have happened if they had stayed partners. Doc replied that it was best not to blame your misfortunes on others.

The sun came back.

Raider talked to the sun.

He cursed it.

He cursed the rawhide that dug into his throat.

He shook with rage and fever, crying out to the buzzards that circled overhead.

He saw Asa Cantrell.

The gunfighter, Johnny Dallas.

He saw Bright Feather. She was cursing him, holding a child in her arms. She was calling him hateful names.

His eyes felt like they were melting out of his head.

He saw Junior Mays standing between him and the sun. He spoke to the man as if they had just met on a busy street. Junior shook his head and bent to cut the rawhide bonds.

"Yessiree," Raider said happily, "that Red Dog staked me out like a raw filly. Left me here t' die."

"You ain't gonna die," Junior Mays replied. "You're just gonna act loco for a while. Maybe longer."

"I hate that fuckin' Injun," Raider said. "If I get my hands on 'im, I'll tear his throat out."

He felt the bonds loosen on his wrists. He lunged for Junior Mays. The deputy marshal dodged him and reached down to cut the rawhide that was wrapped around Raider's feet.

Junior Mays knew that men in a delerium would lash out at the first thing they saw.

"Lucky I came along when I did," Mays said.

Raider just kept making strange noises that he believed to be human speech. He had no idea that he was being saved from Red Dog's torture. It did not occur to the raging big man that Junior Mays was throwing him on the horse to take him east to the Three Forks spread. Raider just figured that the deputy marshal was his ride to the gates of heaven.

CHAPTER THIRTEEN

Raider knew he must be in heaven because he heard the voice of an angel. She was talking to a man, whose voice Raider did not recognize. They were arguing about something. It was only when he woke up and listened to the other two people in the bedroom that he realized they were arguing about him.

"They say he killed two men," the man said. "And he's supposed to be the one that stampeded the herd at the Delta Plain. What if he tries something like that around here?"

The woman had to be Thalia. He had never forgotten the short, forceful way she had of expressing herself. It made you want to do exactly as she said.

"Now you listen to me, Mac Wilson," she started in on her husband. "If Marshal Mays says this man is a Pinkerton agent, then I'm inclined to believe him. When the Pinkerton is better, he can help you with this mess. He can find Red Dog."

Mac Wilson's tone had more than a touch of sarcasm. "Looks like he already did. And where did he end up? Staked out on the plain. Hell, it was a lucky break that Mays found him."

"Don't you swear in this house, Mac!"

"I'm sorry, Thalia."

Raider wanted to sit up, to tell Wilson about Red Dog's hideout. But he found that he was too weak to move. So he had to settle for opening his eyes. It was blurry at first, but then he focused. He saw only Mac Wilson.

The rancher was clean and well-groomed, sporting a big handlebar mustache. Weathered skin, tired blue eyes, sun-streaked hair. He looked familiar, but then Raider figured he had seen a lot of trail hands in his day who looked exactly like Wilson.

Thalia stepped into view, putting her arms around her husband's waist. They embraced and she gave him a sweet kiss. Raider felt his heart beating. He wanted to speak but he could not force the words out of his parched mouth.

"Thalia, you got to trust me," Wilson said to his wife. "We're almost there. This herd is going to make us some real money."

"I love you, Mac. But lately it hasn't felt right on Three Forks."

"It's just the roundup," he insisted.

She broke away. "I suppose. But what if something happens like that stampede over at Delta Plain?"

"I can't control Red Dog," he told her. "Besides, I think Cantrell staged that ruckus to take suspicion away from himself. I know he's working with that Apache. And I'll find proof."

Thalia gestured toward the bed. "Let him help when he's better."

Wilson exhaled impatiently. "Thalia, I've always taken care of my own. I intend to do that now. And this boy better not get in the way. That's the last I have to say on it."

He turned to leave.

"Wilson!"

Raider's voice sounded like the croaking of a ninety-year-old bullfrog.

But the lean rancher turned back to look at him.

"He's awake," Thalia said, reaching for a pitcher.

She poured a glass of water and held it for him. Raider drained the glass and then another. She dabbed his forehead with a wet cloth.

"Got to talk to you, Wilson," Raider said.

The rancher came closer. "Had you pegged for a goner, boy."

Raider nodded feebly. "So did I. Red Dog. He's west o' here. Has stolen cows from both spreads."

Wilson eyed him, shaking his head. "My men combed that ridge country to the west. They didn't find a thing."

"Listen," he mumbled. "Cattle in box canyon. Hidden. Look for the trail. You'll find it."

Wilson smiled, like he was patronizing the big man. "Well,

you just rest on it. When you're better you can show me where you're talkin' about."

Raider tried to sit up. "No!"

Thalia pushed him back down. "You lie still."

"He's ravin'," Mac Wilson said, waving him off.

"You go look!" Raider said in a hoarse voice. "Do it now, before he moves. You'll find them."

Wilson turned without another word and left the room.

Thalia dabbed at Raider's forehead. "Forgive him, Ray. He's had a lot on his mind lately. There ain't been nothin' but trouble since that Cantrell came here. It's been hard on him."

Raider touched her hand. "You called me Ray."

She smiled. "That's your name, isn't it? Ray Howard. Just like it always was. Just like it was when you left me back in Wyoming."

Raider started to cry. She touched his tears with the cloth, but he could see that she was frowning. He couldn't blame her for hating him. And he told her so in a slow, cracking voice.

Thalia lowered her eyes, pulling her hand away from him. "I stopped hating you a long time ago, Ray. I met Mac about two weeks after you went. He was down from Three Forks to buy horses from my father."

"Nobody's called me by my right name in ten years."

She seemed to soften. "I heard about you three times since you left. Once was when you joined up with Mr. Pinkerton. A drummer brought that news along. Another was when you saved the spread over at the Elk Lodge Valley. Johnny Welton rode through here and told us all about it. The third time was when I was in Denver. Some marshal there was talking about all the trouble you made catching some bank robbers."

Raider tried to smile. "How'd you know it was me?"

She stared seriously into his face. "How many men you know got black eyes in their heads?"

"I want t' help your husband, Thalia."

She touched his hand. "I hope you can, Ray. I been feeling bad lately, but I feel better now that you come. I know you can give Mac a hand."

Raider sank back into the pillow. He couldn't think of anything else to say. She fed him cold water until he thought he was going to float off. She also dabbed ointment on his blotches of sun poisioning. She said the spots weren't too bad, that they'd probably clear up if he kept them covered and stayed out of the sun.

That evening, Mac Wilson came into Raider's room and sat by the bed. He inquired as to how Raider was feeling and then started his dialogue. He was a terse man, used to coming to a point and then not expecting to be challenged on it once he got there.

"There ain't no cows in that box canyon, Mr. Howard."

Raider sighed. "Call me Ray, sir."

"All right, Ray. It don't make no never mind what you want to be called. We rode all afternoon till we found the path you was talkin' about. There was a canyon there, hidden behind the ridge. But there wasn't no cattle there."

"Red Dog moved them," Raider said weakly. "I got t' get outta this bed and go after him."

Wilson stopped him. "Hold on, boy. I'd say it was a good sign that Red Dog has cleared out. He got what he came for and now he's gone. Probably gonna run them cattle up to Canada, though I don't know who that crazy Apache is gonna sell 'em to up there."

Raider turned to regard his host. "How you know Red Dog is an Apache?"

Wilson rubbed his mustache. "What?"

"You said twice that Red Dog was Apache."

"I reckon I heard you sayin' it in your sleep," Wilson replied. "You was rantin' somethin' fierce when they brought you in. Mostly you was cursin' that damned Apache."

Raider nodded. "I hope the talk weren't too rough on the women folk."

Wilson smiled and chuckled. "I reckon Mr. Pinkerton does hire gentlemen after all." He rose and started to leave.

"Mr. Wilson."

"Yes, Ray?"

Raider drew a long breath. "Thank you for puttin' me up here. I'll see that you're paid for your trouble."

Wilson shrugged. "You can't pay for all the trouble I got, partner."

"Then I'm gonna stay and help you put things right."

"No need," Wilson replied. "I can handle it from here. I think we seen the last of Red Dog."

"What about the Delta Plain?" Raider challenged.

Wilson frowned. "That ain't your never-mind."

"The terr'torial gover'ment seems t' think different. They hired me t' come in here an' find out what was really goin' on. You wouldn't want t' stand in the way o' that, would you?"

Wilson pointed a finger to the west. "It's a long way to Helena, Mr. Howard. I don't see nobody tellin' me what to do."

"I gotta stay on," Raider said. "It's my job."

Wilson scowled at him, taking a step back toward the bed. "There wouldn't be another reason you're so set on stayin', would there?"

Raider felt uneasy. "Like what?"

"Like my wife."

Raider lowered his eyes. "She told you 'bout me?"

"Ever'thing. How you run away. But I can't say I hold that agin you 'cause Thalia is mine now. You made that possible. But it wouldn't be right you're stayin' on here."

Raider looked straight at him, his eyes glinting in the white light of a half-dozen candles. "Then I'll find another place t' stay, Mr. Wilson. But I ain't leavin' this terr'tory till I round up Red Dog an' his gang."

Wilson did not seem to hear what Raider was saying. He leaned closer to the bed, staring straight into the big man's eyes. Raider had not expected the move and was completely taken aback at the man's boldness.

"Eyes black as coal," Wilson said. "She never told me that."

He wheeled and walked out quickly.

Raider wasn't sure what had happened.

But then, the next morning, everything came quickly into focus.

Thalia brought him a big tray of pancakes for breakfast. Raider thought he wasn't hungry, at least until the first bite. He had polished off the whole stack before Thalia could pour his coffee.

"I feel better t'day," he told her. "My voice is comin' back. It don't even hurt t' sit up."

She nodded and began to dab his wrists with ointment.

"Mac lit out o' here pretty quick last night," Raider offered.

Thalia sighed, wiping the ointment from her fingers. "He went over to Ekalaka this mornin'. Said he was going to meet with some men. I hope they ain't gunslingers."

Raider's eyes narrowed. "He don't seem to fear Cantrell much. And he thinks Red Dog is gone. Darn. Maybe Cantrell *is* the one who's causin' all the grief. But why would he let me go?"

"What?"

Raider smiled. "Nothin'."

She lifted the tray and started toward the door.

"I hear y'all got a pup," Raider called to her. "A boy."

The tray crashed on the floor. Thalia turned to him with a hateful gleam in her eyes. He had said the wrong thing. She was going to try to keep it from him, but he could read her expression.

"Damn your black eyes, Ray Howard. Why'd you have to mention it? Ain't you got a lick of sense in your head after all these years?"

That said, she stormed out of the room, leaving the mess on the floor.

Raider had seen her hot temper before, although it had never been directed at him. He wanted to get up and clean the mess from the dropped tray, but when he spun his legs off the bed, he became lightheaded and nearly fainted. He put his head back on the pillow and the dizziness went away.

By that time, Thalia was back and she had a boy with her.

"Ray Howard, I want you to meet somebody," she said in a calm tone. "This is my son, Robert Wilson. You wanted to see the Pinkerton, Bobby. Well, there he is."

Raider nodded politely at the boy who stood before him.

Bobby Wilson was a lanky, dark-haired, big-boned boy of fifteen or sixteen. He had not filled out yet, although he was wiry and seemed to be hardened from ranch work.

Raider held out his hand. "Come here, boy. I won't bite."

Bobby stepped forward to shake his hand. "I'm pleased, sir. Pleased as I can be."

"My name ain't sir, Bobby. Tell you what, you can call me Raider. How's that? A lot of people call me . . ."

Raider looked into his face for the first time. The boy was close enough for him to see the trait that gave it away, why Thalia was so angry. It had been clear to Mac Wilson the night before.

"What's wrong?" Bobby asked. "I didn't do nothin' to spook you, did I?"

"No, boy, you didn't."

Raider couldn't stop staring at the kid's eyes. Ebony irises stared back at him; eyes as dark as his own.

"Are you all right?" Bobby asked.

Raider nodded.

"You turned plum white," the kid insisted. "Here take some water."

Raider had two glasses of water before he looked over Bobby's shoulder, searching for Thalia.

But she had left the room.

It was just him and the kid and those black eyes, staring down at him from a friendly, familiar face.

Raider had to get out of bed. After the kid was gone, he put his feet on the floor. He walked a few steps to a closet where he found a thick robe to cover his body. He didn't know where Thalia was, but he was going to find her if he had to search every room in the house.

She was in the kitchen, cleaning up the breakfast dishes.

Raider came in and stood behind her. She did not look back, but she knew he was there. Her back was stiff, like she was going to resist. He couldn't blame her.

"I had that comin'," he said softly.

Suddenly she turned and flew toward him, wrapping her arms around his waist, sobbing. "Oh, Ray, I'm sorry. I didn't want to do it like that. I wanted to keep it from you."

"I had it comin'," he repeated.

She felt good against him. It made the ache go deeper to the bone. A man's sins didn't come back on him everyday, but when they did, it was almost more than he could bear.

"Then Bobby's mine?" he asked softly.

Thalia drew back. "You can't tell him," she pleaded. "No one else must ever know."

Raider lowered his head. "I think Mac figgered it out last night when he saw my eyes were the same color as Bobby's."

"I never told him I was pregnant, Ray. We got married so quick, he just figured it was his. Last night, he told me he knew you were Bobby's father. But he said it didn't matter. He just wanted to forget it and never speak of it again."

Raider felt weak. "Your husband's a good man." He had to sit down.

"Here," Thalia said, "take some more water."

After he drank, he looked at her. "Thalia, this is loco, me showin' up here an' you bein' in the middle o' all this. I can't help but feel that there's a reason I'm here. Maybe I'm s'posed t' pay you back for the way I left. I never would've gone if I knew you had a baby inside you."

She blushed. "I thought of that many times. I knew you didn't know, but I still hated you for a long while. But I had a whole lot of years up here to think it over. I reckon in my own way, I was as foolish as you."

"That still don't make it right, my leavin'."

"No," she replied sadly, "it doesn't make it right."

"I want to," Raider offered. "I want to clear the slate, settle up my debt."

She leaned toward him over the kitchen table. "Then stop all this fightin' between Cantrell and my husband."

He nodded. "All right."

Thalia frowned. "Just like that, you think you can stop it."

Raider exhaled. "No, not just like that. But there are things that can be done. I ain't never failed a case in my whole life as a Pink."

She smiled. "There's still some of the man left that I used to know."

He tried to touch her hand.

She pulled back. "Just stop the fightin', Ray. We need this roundup. I want to send Bobby back east to school. I don't want him livin' the rough life forever."

Raider wanted to say that the rough life could do all right by a man, but he decided such a comment might bring on

Thalia's ire. He realized that he had always avoided proper women after Thalia, because of their unpredictable dispositions. His mouth always got him in trouble.

"Get back to bed," Thalia told him. "You can at least get your strength back before you settle all this trouble. I'll find you something to wear besides that robe."

Raider felt his sadness diminishing a little. He stood again, thinking it might be at least another day before he could walk well. Maybe two. "What are you going to do?" Thalia asked bluntly.

He started for his bed. "We'll talk about it when your husband gets back from Ekalaka."

But Mac Wilson did not come back the next day.

Raider woke to find that he could get out of bed with only a minor aching in every cell of his body. He asked Thalia if there was a local medicine man and she said that there wasn't a doctor for miles. He told her he wanted an Indian witch doctor. She replied that the man who handled their remuda was a Crow half-breed named Rich Elk. Rumor had it that Rich Elk knew Indian magic.

Raider walked toward the Three Forks stables, finding the Indian in the middle of a shoeing job.

When Raider asked Rich Elk if he could make an Indian tonic, the half-breed replied that he would do it if Raider would help him finish the shoeing. Raider agreed and assisted the man as he shod the troublesome filly. When they were finished, the Indian went into a storeroom and pulled out a bottle of a thick, black liquid.

"Already had it made," Rich Elk said. "Never seen a white man take much stock in an Injun cure."

Raider grinned. "I don't know if you've noticed, Rich Elk, but there ain't too many smart ones among us white folks."

"I certainly agree with that."

"You got a cup?"

Raider drained off three slugs of the Indian brew and went back to the house. He slept for a long time, only to wake up with someone hovering over his bed. When he opened his eyes, the kid started to run away.

"Hey!" Raider called. "Come back here."

Bobby Wilson lowered his head and slunk back like a hangdog.

"Don't slouch, boy," Raider said.

Bobby stood up straight.

"That's right."

Raider couldn't believe it. His own son standing in front of him. The big man hadn't known his own father too well.

Was it really true?

"How you feelin', Mr. Howard?"

"I thought you was gonna call me Raider."

"Raider..."

The big man stretched. "Damn...I mean, dang. I feel a lot better. That Injun brew did the trick. I gotta find out what they put in there some day an' try t' sell it."

Bobby laughed.

Raider glared at him. "What's so danged funny?"

Bobby shrugged. "I don't know. Just the way you said it just now."

"Oh yeah? And how'd I say it?"

"Like you didn't care what anybody else in the world thought about it. You just said it. Free-like."

Raider laughed and got off the bed. "Yeah, I reckon that's the way I am. Sometimes it gets me in trouble."

"I know what you mean," Bobby replied. "It happens to me all the time. One minute I'm goin' along fine, then, boom, the next minute I'm ass-deep in trouble with my paw or my maw."

"Don't say ass, boy."

"Yes, sir."

Raider eyed the kid, wondering if it was really true. "How old are you, Bobby?"

"Be sixteen next November."

Raider counted the years and decided it had to be so.

He saw that the kid was staring at him. "What's on your mind, boy? How come you was standin' over me like that?"

Bobby blushed and, for a moment, Raider saw Thalia in him. But then he straightened up and looked Raider right in the eye. He had gotten that from Mac Wilson. It hurt Raider that another man had raised his son. He knew from experience that looking back and having regrets could drive you crazy.

This was tougher, though, than anything he had ever dealt with before. It was plain damned agony. It hurt even more that it was all his fault.

"Paw always says if you got somethin' to say, just say it," replied young Bobby. "Here, let me show you somethin'."

He took a package from under the bed. It was something wrapped in oilcloth. Bobby unrolled the cloth to reveal an old percussion Navy Colt. The pistol was rusted and dirty.

"Maw don't know that I got it," Bobby offered. "I told Paw that I found it in the barn. I also showed it to him. He said it didn't matter as long as I didn't shoot nobody."

"Can't shoot this unless you clean it up."

Bobby smiled enthusiastically. "I was hopin' you'd help me. Paw don't have much time since we started roundup."

Raider took the Navy from the kid. "Meet me in back o' the stable in one hour."

"Yes sir!"

He ran out like he had just heard of a gold strike.

Raider looked at the Colt. Thalia wouldn't like him showing the kid how to use a gun. But it was a skill Bobby would need all his life. Montana wasn't getting much tamer, despite what people said. Maybe that was why all of this stuff had come back to haunt him.

If nothing else, he could teach the kid to shoot. It was one thing the big man from Arkansas knew how to do. And he could do it well, as he recalled.

"Where'd you get that gun?" asked Bobby Wilson.

Raider hefted an Army Colt that he had borrowed from the half-breed livery man. "Let's just say I gotta shoe a bunch o' horses till your paw . . . till Mac Wilson gets back."

Bobby looked sort of sad. "Where'd you put my gun?"

"I couldn't get it in workin' order, Bobby. Here, we'll have t' make do with this."

He handed Bobby the Colt. The kid hefted the weight of it. Raider squinted at the way he balanced it in the palm of his hand.

"Here, kid. I brought some bottles from the house. Had to pull teeth t' get your maw t' give 'em t' me."

He walked out away from the stable, putting the bottles in

a row on the ground, about ten of them. That should be enough, he thought. Besides, Rich Elk had only wanted to part with ten cartridges, which would be enough to let the kid plunk off a few errant rounds. Raider doubted that he would break a bottle with each slug.

When the bottles were in place, he walked back and took the gun from Bobby. "Now shootin' a pistol is diff'rent than a rifle. You don't use your sights, not really. It's like pointin' with your finger, only the barrel of the gun is your finger. You listenin'?"

"Yes, sir."

"Point and shoot," Raider said. "Rich Elk said this piece shoots a little to the high side, so I'll aim for the bottom o' one o' those bottles. Look here. I'm sportin' five shots, with the hammer restin' on an empty chamber. Why you think that is?"

Bobby thought about it then replied: "To keep from shootin' off a bullet by accident."

"Good," Raider said. "Now watch me."

The big man raised the Colt and fired off a quick burst that shattered the first bottle in the row.

"Hot dang!" Bobby cried. "That was great!"

Raider handed him the gun. "Here, you try it."

Bobby started to cock the Colt and fire immediately.

"Hold on," Raider urged. "You gotta relax, t' be steady. Let your hands an' your eyes do all the work. If you can point at it, you can hit it."

The kid closed his eyes for a second and took a deep breath. When he opened his eyes again, he had a strange expression on his young face. Raider saw a familiar gleam in his black eyes.

Bobby raised the Army, fired one shot and burst the second bottle in the line. He couldn't believe he had hit it. His mouth was agape.

"Were you shootin' at the second one?" Raider asked.

"Yes, sir."

"Try it again, boy."

Bobby fired too quickly the second time, missing the third bottle.

Raider told him to steady himself before the next shot.

Bobby stood still and then raised the gun, firing, shattering the third bottle to bits.

He was a natural. Raider had been the same way. Any doubts that he had about Bobby being his son were erased forever.

He told Bobby to put the gun in his belt, to draw fast and try to hit any one of the bottles.

On the third pull, Bobby hit his mark. He drew again and hit another one. He would have hit them all, had he not run out of shells.

"Hey, Mr. Howard, I did pretty good, didn't I?"

He turned to see Raider staring at him with his dark eyes. He wondered why the Pinkerton didn't say anything. He just turned away from Bobby and walked back to the ranch house, leaving the kid to return the Army Colt to Rich Elk.

CHAPTER FOURTEEN

Raider didn't want to think about the boy anymore. He was numb, inside and out. He took supper early, to avoid seeing Bobby. Thalia was silent as she served him in the kitchen. She seemed to be spent as well, like everything had been drained out of her.

"I think I'll go help Rich Elk with the shoeing," Raider said to her when he had finished eating.

She just nodded, letting him go without a word.

Raider stepped out of the house, stopping to feel the evening breeze on his face. It was a quiet place. Raider's eyes opened wider. He listened, but could not hear a single noise from the ranch. Thalia was no longer making noise in the kitchen and Rich Elk's livery was quiet.

As he strode toward the stable, Raider realized that he had not seen one cow since he had arrived at the Three Forks spread. Nor had he seen a crew of any kind, with the exception of Rich Elk. The remuda was not even a large one, consisting of twenty or thirty horses. He had known trail drives to take on a hundred and fifty mounts and that was for a small remuda. Cantrell sported at least two hundred horses for the trail drive south.

Mac Wilson had mentioned a herd to his wife, saying the cattle were going to pay off big. But where were the holding pens? And the hands? An empty bunkhouse sat darkly to the left of the stable. He had seen no lights there the night before, but it had not struck him as odd until now.

Wilson was behind if he planned to round up his herd and get it moving south before September. Raider knew from experience that most Montana ranchers got their roundup started in the spring. Cantrell was on schedule. Maybe the red-haired man really was stealing Mac Wilson's cows and keeping them for his own herd.

The gunslinger, Johnny Dallas, had insisted the Delta Plain hands were cutting out Three Forks steers and driving them north. But that could have been a ruse. Just like setting him free. They could be playing it close, hoping Raider got caught in the crossfire. What did one Pink matter if Cantrell had the guns and the herd? Killing Raider could have brought him a lot more trouble than rustling a few steers.

Yet Marshal Mays had said that both sides were gearing up for a confrontation. But where were Wilson's hands? Maybe Cantrell was spreading poison, infecting the marshal's ears with lies. If Cantrell could paint Wilson to be the villain, then the red-haired man might be able to attack the Three Forks spread and get away with it. After all, local sentiment ran with Wilson. Maybe the locals were right.

"You gonna help me with this pony? Or you just gonna stand there starin' into space?"

Rich Elk stood in the stable, wrestling with the hoof of a bitchy mare.

Raider went to help him, his mind still turning.

What if Wilson had ridden to Ekalaka to hire more guns?

The big man shook his head. He had to stop thinking like that. True, Wilson had been sort of rude to him. But that was the tension from Raider's past with Thalia. And it had to hurt to know another man fathered your child. Raider was surprised that Wilson hadn't shot him when he found out. A lesser man would have been driven to violence.

The mare tried to move.

Rich Elk looked up at Raider. "Are you gonna hold her?"

Raider tightened his grip on the mare. "Sorry."

Rich Elk wiped his brow. "Don't worry about it. This is the last one. Then I'm finished for the day." He started to drive the nails into the mare's hoof.

Raider decided to sound out the half-breed, who seemed to be the only hand on Three Forks. "Kind of a small remuda ain't it?"

The Indian laughed. "Small for what?"

"For takin' a herd south. That's a long ride. Can't have more than two dozen horses here."

Rich Elk put in the last nail and then looked up. "I don't see any herd. D'you?"

"Wilson seems to think he's got one. Told his wife that it was going to pay off big."

Rich Elk laughed again. "Well, there might be a herd out there somewhere. This is a big country. But I haven't seen one."

Raider moved aside, watching as Rich Elk put his tools away.

"Some say Cantrell is stealing Wilson's cows," Raider offered. "And the Indian Red Dog is workin' with Cantrell."

"Well," Rich Elk replied. "I wouldn't be surprised."

Raider squinted at the half-breed. "Look here, Rich Elk, you don't seem too int'rested in anything that's goin' on round this territory."

"No, I suppose not."

"Why? Ain't it excitin' enough for you?"

Rich Elk sighed, a low, defeated chortle that Raider had heard from other Indians. "I just want to draw my back wages and get the hell out of here. Nothin' else of it has anythin' to do with me. Savvy?"

The sound of horses arriving interrupted their conversation.

Mac Wilson rode in with two men riding behind him. Even in the dim light of dusk, Raider could tell they were shootists. They had the lean, wary look and their guns were worn low. Wilson had brought in his own soldiers for the range war.

"You still here?" Wilson asked Raider.

"I was just helpin' Rich Elk with some shoein'."

Raider gestured toward the livery man but he was no longer there.

"It's about time for you to leave," Wilson said as he dismounted.

The gunmen got out of their saddles as well.

Raider felt naked without a gun.

Wilson eyed him with a look that would have frozen a weaker man. "Where'd you get my clothes?" he asked.

Raider shrugged, trying to be friendly. "I reckon Thalia give 'em t' me. They're a little short on me, but I ain't one t' complain."

"Seems you like things that ain't yours, Pinkerton. That can be dangerous in a territory like this."

Raider just stood there, waiting to see what the gunmen were going to do.

But Wilson waved the men toward the house. "My wife'll get grub for you. Go on, I'll be all right."

After shooting hostile looks toward Raider, the two men walked back toward the house.

"Couple o' rough ones there," Raider said. "Best watch your back."

Wilson pointed a finger at him. "I want you out of here, Pinkerton. You hear me? Tonight."

"Best let me stay an' help," Raider offered. "Don't seem like you got too many men backin' you up."

"My crew's on the range," Wilson said. "Roundin' up my cows."

Raider tried to ignore Wilson's hateful expression. "It ain't no sin t' have trouble with a ranch, Wilson. If you need a hand, I'm willin' t' help. I can . . ."

"There wasn't any trouble here until you came!" the rancher retorted.

Raider nodded. "Okay, I'll go. I need t' buy a horse from you. I don't have any money but I'll see that you get it."

"You're walkin'," Wilson replied. "I can't spare the mount."

"Walkin'? In the middle o' the night?"

Wilson chortled disgustedly. "Be thankful I don't take the clothes off your back."

Raider started toward the stable door. "I want t' say good-bye to Thalia afore I go."

Wilson drew a sidearm and pointed it at the big man's gut. "No farewells. You left her before without saying good-bye. You can do it again."

"That ain't fair, Wilson."

"It ain't supposed to be. Now you clear out, Pinkerton. Take your black eyes and leave Three Forks before I decide to kill you."

Mac Wilson turned away and stormed back to his house.

As soon as he was gone, Rich Elk came back into the

stable, entering from a side door. "I did not like the look of those men with Wilson," he said to Raider.

The big man scoffed. "Hell, somethin' finally got your attention."

Rich Elk shook his head. "I won't make you walk. There's a mule back there. No saddle, though."

Raider looked toward the house, hoping to catch a glimpse of Thalia or the boy. "He's bringin' in his own gunhands. Rich Elk, was that true what he said about havin' men in the field gatherin' his cows?"

The half-breed shrugged. "There were a half-dozen men here a while back. They left though. Some more men rode in after that, but I don't think Wilson hired them. They were gone the next day."

Raider saw Thalia pass by the window. She did not stop to look out toward the stable. She couldn't very well go against her husband after he told Raider to leave. The big man felt sad and empty. But that just stiffened his resolve to capture Red Dog and uncover the real truth. If nothing else, he was going to make sure Thalia and Bobby lived in a peaceful place.

"Here," Rich Elk said, handing something to Raider.

He took the Army Colt from the half-breed's hand.

"I've only got about thirty cartridges left, but you can have them."

Raider nodded appreciatively. "Thanks."

"You shot pretty good," Rich Elk said. "So did the boy."

"I'll pay you for this or return it," Raider replied. "Same with the mule. I'm good for the money."

Rich Elk shrugged. He told Raider not to worry, that he had a rifle and a scattergun for protection. He also apologized for the mule, but added that it was his to give, while the other horses in the remuda belonged to Wilson.

Raider thanked him and started to lead the mule out into the yard.

"One more thing," Rich Elk said.

Raider looked back to see him offering the jug of Indian medicine.

"Take a slug for the trail, cowboy."

Raider obliged him, draining some of the thick, dark liquid. "You've been a big help, Rich Elk. I thank you."

"Got to like a man who trusts Injun medicine."

Raider rolled onto the bare back of the mule. It was going to be a long ride. He thought about riding next to the kitchen window, to get one more look at Thalia before he left, but he knew the two gunmen would be in the kitchen, eating. He did not want to have a shootout with them. Wilson was too hot and Raider didn't want to make trouble.

He turned the mule toward the east, plodding off into the approaching night. . . .

Raider intended to ride the mule to Tinker's store and get directions to the nearest telegraph wire. But he never got there. He had been riding for about ten minutes when he became aware that someone was following him. One rider. Maybe one of the hired guns that Wilson had brought in.

The big man dropped off the mule and slapped it forward. Then he crouched low, waiting in the darkest shadows as the rider approached. It was an old trick and he half-expected his pursuer to rein up if he had heard Raider hit the ground. But the man kept coming.

Raider got a running start, leaping up to knock the rider from his saddle. He thudded against the ground with Raider on top of him. Raider brought up the Army Colt and stuck it in the kid's face.

"Don't hurt me, mister!" cried Bobby Wilson.

Raider got up, wedging the gun in his pants. "What the hell are you doin' followin' me? Didn't your ma teach you better?"

Bobby was reluctant to get up, fearing that Raider might hit him again. "Maw sent me, Raider. She told me to bring stuff to you."

Raider extended his hand, helping the boy off the ground. "Sorry I tackled you like that. You okay?"

"Yeah, I'm pretty tough."

"Better catch your mount," the big man offered.

"No need," Bobby replied. "Watch this."

The boy whistled and his sorrel gelding came running to him out of the shadows.

"I raised him from a colt," the boy said. "He's fast."

Bobby pulled a rifle from the scabbard on his sling ring.

"Here. Maw sent you this. It's an old Henry rifle. It's loaded full, but that's all the shells we had."

Raider thanked him and took the weapon.

"Here's some food, too," Bobby said. "Maw didn't want you to go hungry. She said to tell you to stick to your promise to stop all this trouble."

"Tell her I will."

Bobby turned away, lowering his head. "I don't like them men that come home with Paw. They ain't very mannerly."

"Aw, don't fret none. Your paw is just tryin' t' protect what's his. Don't forgit, it's yours, too. You'll be the head man o' Three Forks someday. It'll be your ranch then."

"Maw wants me to go back east, to school."

Raider wanted to explain to him how women sometimes got some notion in their heads and they wouldn't let it go no matter what, even if the notion didn't have a hope of working out. But he could not say anything against the boy's mother, so he simply said that Thalia knew best. It would work out if Bobby just gave it a chance.

"Thanks," the boy said. "Nobody ever talks to me like that."

There was an awkward silence. Raider wanted to ask the boy some questions about Three Forks: about the roundup which didn't seem to be happening, about the state of Mac Wilson's affairs.

But the commotion stopped him from asking.

The boy heard it too. "What is it?"

"Cattle," Raider replied. "Headin' west in the dark."

Heading for the box canyon, Raider thought. Maybe that was the way they were doing it. Running cattle in all directions to confuse everyone, then swinging the stolen beef back to the same spot.

"There's about forty head," Raider told the boy. "Is that sorrel of yours really fast?"

Bobby nodded. "He won the hands race two years ago."

"I need to borrow him."

"But . . ."

"That mule won't get it, kid. But if you say no I won't take your horse. Not if you don't want me to."

Bobby looked nervous. "What if I let you take him?"

Raider sighed. "I can't promise there won't be more trouble. But I might get closer to stoppin' it if I can get some answers."

"Take him," Bobby said. "Try not to hurt him if you can help it."

"I won't," Raider replied, jumping into the saddle. "See if you can find the mule. But don't stray too far. I'll be back soon enough."

Raider spurred the sorrel into the darkness, heading after the small group of steers.

Bobby just watched, wondering what kind of man did things so impulsively. He had never stopped to think why his mother seemed to like the man. Bobby liked him well enough, especially after he showed him how to shoot. But something about the tall Pinkerton scared him. And try as he might, the boy could not figure out what it was that made him nervous in Raider's company.

The boy had been right about the gelding. The horse was sure and fast. Raider rode hard in the direction of the running herd, knowing that the riders who moved the cows could not hear his approach.

When he was sure about the location of the small herd, he swung around to the back, looking for a drag man. There was no moon, so it was impossible to see him. Raider heard the horse, though, whinnying as he approached from the rear.

Raider hated to take a man down from his blind side, but this was a special case. He had to get to the source of the trouble. It was the only thing left for him.

He drew the Army and felt its weight. He didn't want to kill the man, just put him out, but it was hard to judge in the dark. Raider spurred the sorrel, driving closer to the sounds of the hooves.

The man in the saddle never even saw him coming. Raider tapped him at the base of his skull, knocking him forward. Reflexively, the unconscious man hugged the neck of the bay he was riding. Raider grabbed the reins of the bay and pulled it away toward the east. The other riders continued on with their steers.

They'd miss their associate soon enough and come back to

look for him. Raider planned to be long gone by then. He looked at the man slumped in the saddle, hoping he had not clubbed some innocent cow trader coming back from a legitimate buy. Then again, innocent cow traders didn't take their livestock home in the dark.

He started off at a lope, but the man fell off the bay.

Raider had to get down and tie the man on the horse, all the while looking for riders in the dark. No one came. Raider remounted and searched in the night until he found the boy. He felt proud that the kid had caught the mule. The boy did what he was told.

"Who's that?" Bobby asked.

Raider laughed. "I don't know yet. I just had to slow 'im down, get his attention so I can ask 'im a few questions."

Bobby gawked at the body, like it was a corpse. "He don't appear to be feelin' right."

Raider felt a stirring in his gut. He wanted to protect the kid from all the things he thought were going to happen. If he was correct in the explanation he was forming, it was going to be raining pure shit.

"Bobby, I want you t' come along with me."

The kid looked up at him, obviously frightened. But, to Raider's amazement, the boy said, "Okay. I'll ride the mule."

"No. We'll string this one over the mule and you can ride your own mount. I'll take the bay. But we gotta hurry. We gotta go find the marshal."

They transferred the unconscious man to the mule, tying him in place.

Raider mounted the bay. "Come on, boy."

Bobby lifted himself into the saddle. "Where you plan to look for the marshal?"

"Tinker's store, the first place anyway."

Bobby agreed that it was a good idea. He felt strangely elated riding after the Pinkerton. His fears had abated for the time being. But when they came back again, they would be like demons from a fiery hole in the ground.

They rode in about dawn.

Tinker took a shot at them as they approached.

Raider called to the old man. "Damn it, Tinker, it's me.

The Pinkerton. You tryin' to shoot me for takin' your squaws?"

"He never hits anything," Bobby said. "Don't worry."

Tinker came out and looked at them. "Who you got strung across that horse there?"

Raider got down off the bay. "We ain't sure yet. You seen the marshal lately?"

"Yesterday," Tinker replied. "Said he'd be back this way again today. You want to wait for him?"

"Yeah. Listen, Tinker, I'm sorry about them squaws. When they saw Cantrell's boys, they decided t' go with 'em."

Tinker only laughed. "Hell, pardner, you done me a favor. I thought I'd never get rid o' them two." Suddenly he looked up, realizing who was in the saddle of the sorrel. "Dog me if it ain't Robert Wilson himself. Whatchoo doin' ridin' wild asses all over creation with this Pink?"

"I'm helpin' him," Bobby announced proudly.

Raider glared at the boy. "No you ain't. I'm leavin' you here with Tinker after I find the marshal."

Bobby didn't like that, but he accepted it without protest.

Tinker looked worriedly to the horizon. "Gonna be that much trouble, huh? You really think so?"

Raider leaned closer to Tinker. "Not in front o' the boy."

That much trouble, Tinker thought.

"Oh well," the storekeeper said blankly, "it had to come to a head sooner or later."

While Raider waited for the marshal, Bobby went upstairs to sleep.

Tinker cut loose the unconscious rider and brought him into the house. He tied his hands and feet at Raider's urging. The big man wondered if the rider was going to wake up. He hadn't hit the man that hard, although he had swatted him with the momentum of the horse behind his blow.

"He still breathin'?" Raider asked.

Tinker shrugged. "Sorta. You jacked his head pretty good. He may not make it."

"Damn." Another loose end that might not knit. "I hope I didn't kill 'im for nothin'."

"Well, he ain't dead yet."

But he died that afternoon. It all seemed like a waste. The marshal had not come, either.

"Tinker, is there a telegraph wire close by?"

"Not unless you count South Dakota. Have to go back all the way to Rapid City. Long trek on that mule."

Raider eyed the old man. "Tinker, what the hell d' you know about any o' the horse shit that's goin' on round here?"

"Just that I don't want no part of it, hombre. And that's the God's honest truth."

It all seemed pretty hopeless until the kid provided the key.

Bobby came downstairs, rubbing his eyes. He stopped when he saw the dead man. "Is he gone?"

Raider just nodded, thinking that he was finally going to have to admit defeat on this case.

"Hey!" Bobby cried. "That's Sporty lyin' there!"

Raider left the whiskey bottle he had been nursing. "You know this man, Bobby? For sure, I mean?"

The kid shrugged. "Yeah, that's Sporty Jenkins. He rode with my Paw for all last year, when they gathered the herd. Then, when Paw couldn't pay him what he wanted, he disappeared. Remember Sporty, Mr. Tinker? Once in a while he'd come by here to your store."

Tinker came back to get a closer look. "Yep, that's Sporty. Funny, I didn't even recognize him when you rode up. Could be that I just don't like people. I've heard that said about me before."

Raider's eyes were glassy, a strange look on his rugged countenance. "That's it," he said. "That's what I needed."

"What?" Bobby asked.

But the big man from Arkansas just stood there, his face slack like he was thinking of something that was going to take a lot of figuring.

The boy and the old man watched him, waiting for his next move.

CHAPTER FIFTEEN

Raider urged the boy's sorrel gelding through the dusk, heading south for Three Forks. Behind him rode Marshal Junior Mays, who showed up at Tinker's store about an hour after Bobby identified the dead man. The dead one was the missing piece that had fallen into place. Now Raider had to play it right.

"Gonna be dark before we get there," said Junior Mays. "The moon'll mostly be gone too."

Raider shrugged. "That's what I want. You just do your part. Let me worry 'bout the details."

Mays's part involved leading the mule with the dead man propped up in a sitting position. Mays didn't like the idea of leading a dead man. It even had their mounts nervous. Animals knew death and were just as affected by it as men.

"The horses are jumpy," Mays offered.

Raider held the sorrel steady. "Mine ain't. And that mule's either too smart or too stupid t' be shook up."

Mays had been humbled. "Sorry, I just don't know about this plan."

"You liked it good enough back at Tinker's."

Humbled again, Mays decided to shut up. He didn't want to lose face in the Pinkerton's eyes. Every man had doubts when he was going into action, and Mays knew a true man never expressed them. If you started talking, you might talk up defeat before you knew it.

Raider was glad Mays had stopped talking. His stomach was churning as well. He had the Henry rifle and Rich Elk's old Army Colt, but he wondered if it was enough fire power if things didn't go his way. If the bluff failed, shooting might be the only way out.

150

The sorrel held steady to the south.

Raider had been proud of the way the boy wanted to come along. Bobby fought for his right to protect Three Forks, but Raider and the marshal overruled him. The kid had to learn that everything wasn't always going to go his way in life. He had sure shown his courage and determination, though.

Raider could not think of him as a son. He tried, but even with his fondness for the kid, he could not make himself believe it. Had Thalia lied to hurt him? He remembered the kid's shooting and his black eyes. It was the truth, even if he couldn't accept it.

"Gettin' darker," Mays offered.

"It'll be easier in the dark," Raider said. "I doubt Wilson has anybody but those two goons he brought in last night. You just hang back an' do your part."

"I won't let you down, Raider."

"I know you won't, Junior."

Mays's loyalty and ability were not what concerned Raider. It was the risk with Thalia in the ranch house. If she was hurt . . . he couldn't think about it. He had to stay steady, like the sorrel.

What made him put responsibility on himself? He could easily wait and send for more agents to back him up. Mays could even raise a posse. Raider liked doing things his own way because it usually worked.

"Look," Mays said, reining up.

Raider lifted his eyes to the dark horizon.

"That's it," he said.

Beyond them, about a half mile away, the lights of the Three Forks ranch house flickered in the night.

They came in slow, behind the empty bunkhouse. The livery was dark. Raider figured Rich Elk would stay out of any tussle. A smart Indian, the big man thought.

Wilson's two hired guns rested on the porch of the house. Raider couldn't see if they had rifles. It didn't matter. Intending to play his hand from the cover of the livery's north wall.

He looked back at Mays. "This is it, boy."

The marshal nodded.

Raider turned toward the ranch house. "Wilson! Mac Wilson. This is the Pinkerton. I'm callin' you out, Mac Wilson."

Both men on the porch lifted Winchesters, firing at the corner of the livery. Raider reined the sorrel behind the wall and dropped to the ground. Mays worked to steady the mule and his own mount.

Raider hit the dirt, crawling to the corner of the barn. From a prone position, he fired two shots, both of which hit their marks. The men on the porch fell to the ground, shaking with death.

Mays couldn't believe the shooting had stopped so quickly. "Did you hit 'em, big man?"

"Yeah, I got 'em."

He stood up, peering toward the house. Thalia appeared for a second in the window upstairs. Someone pulled her away from the casement. Then Wilson looked out himself.

"Wilson!" Raider hollered. "I'm talkin' t' you. Come out on the porch. I won't hurt you if you come peaceable."

They waited for a few minutes before Mac Wilson opened the front door and came onto the porch, a Winchester crooked in his arm.

"You took my boy, Pinkerton," Wilson hollered back. "But you ain't gettin' Thalia."

Raider could drop him with one shot, but he held back. "Wilson, I been thinkin'," he called from the cover of the barn wall, "you know more about all the doin's in this country than you let on."

Wilson rattled the Winchester, fired a shot and then rolled out into the darkness himself.

"What's he doin'?" Mays asked.

Raider told him to hush up. He had to listen for the rancher's movements. Wilson was hunkered down now, ready for a fight in the dark.

"You're hurtin', Wilson," Raider challenged. "Your ranch is goin' downhill. You can't even afford to pay a crew."

"You're so all-fired smart!" Wilson cried from the shadows.

Raider urged Mays away from the barn. "He's circlin'. Let's get on the other side."

"I don't like this, Raider," Mays offered.

Raider grunted a fearful laugh. "You think I do?"

A shot rang out from the darkness, splintering the wood next to Raider's head.

"Keep movin'," he told Mays. "I'm goin' out t' get 'im."

He estimated Wilson's position and started to circle toward the rancher. "I'm smart enough t' figger out that you got a lot t' gain by runnin' Cantrell off this range," he called as he stalked Thalia's husband.

"Cantrell's stealin' my cows," came the echoing reply.

"He's turnin' your steers back toward your land," Raider bellowed. "He also had me caught an' let me go. He wouldn'ta done that if he had somethin' t' hide."

Raider stopped dead for a moment. He wondered if Wilson was still moving. He didn't want to kill the rancher if he could help it. Because of Thalia. She deserved to see her husband get a fair trial.

"You're workin' with Red Dog!" Raider said to the shadows.

A pause, then: "How you figure that, Pinkerton?"

"You knew right off Red Dog was an Apache," the big man replied. "I don't believe you heard me rantin'."

"Even if it's the truth?"

Raider took a few steps and then got low again. "You said you an' your men checked that box canyon west o' here, where Red Dog is keepin' his stolen cattle. You said there weren't no cows there, only I caught some o' your men takin' a small herd that way last night."

"I ain't got no men," Wilson cried. "They all run off 'cause I couldn't pay 'em. Winter was hard on me. I did lose most of my cows. But I ain't workin' with Red Dog."

Raider knew Wilson had stopped, so he stayed put, anticipating a rush from the shadows. "Your men stampeded Cantrell's herd," the big man shouted. "I saw their tracks, followed them south. Only they turned west. Headin' back for Three Forks. The same day your wife came to see Cantrell. Smart move, sending Thalia like that. Made you look like you wanted peace."

"I do, Pinkerton. I swear to the Almighty in heaven. I never sent Thalia, she done that on her own."

She always was a stubborn one, Raider thought.

"Where's my boy?" Wilson cried.

"Safe. He's at Tinker's. Don't worry."

"I don't care if he was your seed, Ray Howard. He'll always be my boy."

Did he hear the man softening? "And I ain't here to dispute that . . ."

A shot rang out from Wilson's rifle, sailing over Raider's head. The big man ran again, heading back toward the barn. It looked like he might have to kill Wilson after all.

He stopped and crouched behind an old wagon.

"I never checked that box canyon," Wilson said suddenly. "I lied. I never even went out there to look."

"You're gonna have t' do better than that," Raider replied. "I know you got a crew workin' out there. They're runnin' stolen cattle in every direction t' keep us confused. I gotta hand it t' you, Wilson, it was a good plan while it lasted."

Wilson's Winchester exploded, chopping up the spokes of the wagon wheels. Raider saw the muzzle flash and fired back. His shots were too high, though. He couldn't bring himself to shoot the man. Time for his trump card. It had better work, he thought, or Mac Wilson was dead.

"Wilson! I got a boy with me who says different. Says you're leadin' the gang along with Red Dog. You want t' hear his name?"

"You're lyin'," Wilson cried. He was moving again. "I ain't mixed up with Red Dog. Can't you get that through your thick head?"

He was running back toward the house.

Raider headed toward the front door of the stable, looking for Mays. "Junior, where the hell are you?"

"Right here!"

Mays led the mule out of the stable. Sporty Jenkins, deceased rustler, stared toward the lights of the house with dead-open eyes. Wilson saw him and stopped cold in his path, holding the Winchester with both hands. Raider aimed the Henry rifle at him.

"Drop it, Wilson."

The rancher gaped at the dead man. "It *is* Sporty. Sporty, tell this Pinkerton I ain't done nothin' he said. Sporty!"

"I said drop it," Raider urged. "I don't want t' kill you."

"I'm innocent, I tell you."

Was Wilson considering a shot with the rifle?

Raider kept his eye on the sight of the Henry. "Just drop it an' take your chance with a trial, Wilson."

"I didn't do it! Tell him, Sporty!"

Had the bluff failed?

Raider had expected Wilson to try to shoot the man who could link him to the gang of rustlers led by Red Dog. But Wilson just stood there, asking Sporty Jenkins to clear him. Since Jenkins was riding with Red Dog, Raider expected the cowboy to be connected to his old boss.

"You're wrong, Pinkerton!" Wilson insisted.

"Then drop your rifle," Raider replied. "That's the only thing that's gonna keep me from pluggin' you right now."

"I'm innocent!"

"Prove it. Drop that rifle an' come toward me. If you ain't guilty, no court in this terr'tory is gonna convict you."

"Please . . . please . . ."

Raider heard the steam going out of him. "I mean it, Wilson. You come quiet-like an' nobody'll hurt you."

"It ain't no sin for a man to have rough times," Wilson muttered. "It ain't no sin to have your cattle die in the winter."

Raider's finger tightened on the trigger. "Do or die, Wilson. Are you comin' on foot, or on the back of a horse?"

The Winchester moved in his hands.

Raider hesitated. "Wilson!"

The rancher dropped the Winchester into the dirt.

Raider couldn't believe it. "Careful," he told Mays. "It may be a trick."

Raider took one step toward Wilson before the rifle exploded. It was the loud report of a buffalo gun, a Sharps probably. Only it wasn't shooting at Raider or the marshal.

Mac Wilson's body jerked and fell to the ground. He lay there, moaning, holding his shoulder. Raider and Mays pulled back into the barn.

They heard the laughter peeling out of the ranch house.

"Who the hell is that?" asked Junior Mays.

"Red Dog," Raider replied.

He knew that laugh all too well.

CHAPTER SIXTEEN

Red Dog was standing on the roof of Wilson's house.

Raider levered the Henry rifle and fired at the Indian, but he vanished as quickly as a gobbler during hunting season. Raider started out of the barn, only to be met by more rifle fire from the darkness.

He ducked back into the livery. "Damn. Red Dog's got 'is men with 'im. And they ain't here for the Saturday night square dance."

Mays was leaning against a horse stall, holding his pistol. "How many you reckon there are?"

"Near as I can figger he's got about ten or twelve men. Had two groups fleecin' both herds."

Mays looked worried. "And you think Wilson is in on it?"

Raider grunted. "I did till just now. But not anymore."

"Maybe Red Dog shot him to make it look good."

The big man shook his head. "No, Wilson was comin' in of his own free will. He was surrenderin' t' me. That's enough."

"Why'd he hire them two gunhands?"

More gunfire, slugs cutting through the stable. The dead figure of Sporty Jenkins caught a couple of rounds and fell off the mule. It wouldn't be long before Red Dog and his men closed in on them.

"Wilson was as scared as anyone when it came t' Red Dog," Raider replied. "My guess is that the Injun offered him a chance t' throw in, but he turned 'im down. I reckon he thought Cantrell had accepted the Apache's offer. That's why he accused 'im o' stealin' ever'body's cows."

Mays looked perplexed, like he could not understand how

156

Raider had figured these things out. "So Cantrell ain't part of it neither?"

"Not as far as I can tell, Junior. But then, I was wrong 'bout Wilson. Still, Cantrell let me go free when he could've hung me high. That's gotta count for somethin'."

More gunfire, this time from rifles that were closer.

"We gotta get out o' here," Raider said. "Let's run out the back in different directions. You head for Tinker's, see if you can raise a posse."

Mays frowned. "What are you gonna do?"

Raider looked back toward the house. "I'm gonna try to get the woman outta there an' maybe kill some o' Red Dog's boys while I'm at it."

Mays thought that sounded risky. Raider told him to shut up and head for the back. With that, the big man fired a couple of rounds to cover the marshal. But it didn't matter. Mays got up, took two steps and then fell dead with a bullet hole in his back. The rifles were close enough to do some damage. Raider had to get the hell out of the barn.

No way to go out through either door.

Raider rolled to the north wall, lying on his back, kicking, splintering two planks, easing out into the night.

Someone rushed him headlong.

Raider fired the Henry rifle at the shadow.

The man screamed that he was hit, squirming like a dog.

Raider left him on the ground, and ran through the darkness.

Two men were standing over the body of Mac Wilson, who seemed to be alive. One of the men had a pistol in his hand, aiming it down at the fallen rancher. Raider fired the Henry, killing the man instantly. He lurched forward, holding a bloody hole in his throat.

The second man raised his weapon.

Raider squeezed the trigger of the Henry, only to have the hammer fall harmlessly on an empty chamber.

The second man fired his pistol, whizzing a slug past the big man's head.

Raider drew the Army Colt from his pants and shot the second gunman in the chest.

The man twitched, stumbling forward, gurgling on his own blood.

When he fell, Raider rushed the bodies, picking up both pistols from the dead man.

Wilson looked up at him. "You saved me."

Raider grabbed him by the collar of his shirt. "We ain't got time for talk, honcho."

He dragged the rancher out of the glow that came from the house lights.

"Hold it right there, Pinkerton!"

Raider fired at the voice that rose out of the shadows.

Another gunman hollered that he was hit, dancing around on one leg. Raider's bullet had caught him in the thigh. When Raider saw him, he fired again, sending two slugs into his heart.

The man fell dead, still moving as the life went out of him.

Wilson coughed. "What's goin' on?"

"Red Dog decided t' make a call."

He dragged the rancher across the yard, toward the dark bunkhouse.

Rifle levers chortled in the night. "Stop it right there, Pinkerton."

Raider hesitated. He couldn't see them clearly, but he knew there were three riflemen. They were spreading out behind him, coming in from different directions. Even if he got off three shots, he would never hit all three of them before they shot him.

"Drop it," another voice commanded.

Raider had to let go of the Army Colt, dropping it on the ground next to Wilson. He also dropped the weapons of the dead men that he had picked up. The riflemen moved in, keeping their distance. A Pinkerton was a man to be reckoned with, to be respected as someone who could kill you without a moment's hesitation.

"Hey, that's ol' Wilson there," a third man said.

"Lookin' pretty dead to me."

"Yeah, he shoulda gone in with us when we joined Red Dog. Wouldn't'a hurt him to lose his herd then."

"Keep your eye on the Pink."

"Hot damn, we got us one."

They were just shapeless voices in the dark.

"Somebody's gotta tie him up."

No one seemed ripe for the task. Finally, the other two men talked the weakest member of the trio into taking the job. As he moved in, Raider turned to glare at him.

"Damn, he looks mean. Y'all come in and help me."

"Let's wait for the others."

"Hell, he's just one man!"

That fact seemed to put them more at ease. After all, what was one unarmed man against three rifles? They came closer, to where Raider could see all three of them.

"Hell, he don't look so tough."

Raider just felt tired. He wondered why they hadn't shot him outright. Maybe Red Dog wanted to torture him again.

"All right, boys," he challenged. "Let's get this over with."

His luck had run out. He fully expected to be bound and taken to the Apache leader. It was sure a long way from Apache country.

He held out his hands for the ropes.

The man approached him cautiously. "He's a big 'un."

The man drew a loop around his wrists.

Then a pistol exploded.

The man with the rope fell to the ground.

Wilson had picked up the Army Colt and had shot him in the gut.

"He shot him!"

Both riflemen were stunned. One of them turned his rifle on Wilson. Raider lashed out with his boot, kicking the rifle out of the man's grasp. Wilson shot the man who was still holding his Winchester. Raider picked up one of the rifles from the ground and shot the man who was reaching for the weapon that had been kicked out of his hands.

Raider grabbed Wilson's collar again. "Come on, boy. We got seven of 'em so far. That'd leave maybe a half dozen, countin' Red Dog."

Raider started dragging him across the yard.

Somewhere a woman screamed in the darkness.

The big man stopped cold. "Thalia."

"The Injun," Wilson moaned. "He's got her."

Raider looked back toward the house, but he could see no movement.

"Go get her," Wilson said. "Don't let him hurt her."

Raider touched the rancher's shoulder, which was sticky with blood. "You need that wound tended to."

"No. Help Thalia. I don't care if I die. Just save her from Red Dog."

Raider felt a sudden surge of anger toward the rancher. "You had t' know Red Dog was usin' your old crew. Why didn't you help the marshal?"

But Wilson only gurgled and passed out. He was still breathing. Raider wondered if the rancher deserved to be alive.

Thalia screamed again.

"That Apache bastard!"

Raider started for the house.

The screams became nonstop, rising with horrific echos that rang across the yard.

He could not go in through the front door. He ran to the side of the house, knowing that he would run into Red Dog's men at any second. Sure enough, as he approached the back, someone rushed him. Raider swung the Army Colt into the man's skull, smashing him, knocking him to the ground, killing him silently.

More men ran in front of the house. They had not heard him. Four of them. They dispersed in different directions to look for him.

Thalia cried out in the house. She was begging the Indian to stay away from her. Raider had heard enough. He had to kill the Apache and do it quickly.

Easing around the side of the house, he started up the back steps. Suddenly all the lights in the house went dark, disappearing one at a time as someone snuffed them out. Raider froze on the porch. Red Dog was playing with him.

"You Apache son of a bitch," he muttered under his breath.

He heard the voice of one of the men, who was calling that he had found the body of Wilson.

Raider stepped into the kitchen.

The air was still and hot inside the house.

Raider paused, holding the Army in front of him, listening. All he needed to hear was the Indian's breathing. If he could mark him, he could kill him.

"Ray!" Thalia cried. "Get out. Leave before he kills you."

Sound of a slap, crisp report of hand on face.

Raider flinched. "Red Dog!"

"Come and get me, white man!"

Raider fought the urge to rush straight into the parlor. He felt each step carefully, anticipating the creak of his feet on floor boards. He had to be cautious because of Thalia.

As he stepped toward the parlor, something made a scratchy sound.

Light flared as a sulphur match ignited.

Raider raised the Army, expecting to get off a shot.

Instead of firing, he froze as Red Dog touched the match to the wick of an oil lamp.

"Hello, Pinkerton," Red Dog said. "I never knew a man to escape from my stakes. But you sure as hell did."

Red Dog was standing next to the lamp. Thalia was in a chair beside him. The Apache had the Sharps cocked and loaded with the bore pressed against Thalia's head. Even if Raider shot him, Red Dog would still be able to fire the rifle and kill Thalia in a second.

"You don't want her to die," Red Dog said.

"No, I don't."

"Then drop the pistol, or I'll splatter her all over the inside of this house." His hateful eyes narrowed. "Do it!"

The Army Colt thudded on the floor.

"Now raise your hands," Red Dog commanded.

Raider scowled, lifting his hands toward the ceiling. "You better kill me, Red Dog. If you don't, I'll put your heart on a stake and roast it over a fire."

The other men rushed in from outside.

"Hey, look," one of them said, gawking, "the boss done got the Pink."

"Red Dog," offered another, "Wilson is still alive. What you want us to do with him?"

"Keep him alive," Red Dog replied. "We're going to have

a little hanging party tomorrow morning at dawn."

"You gonna hang the woman too?" someone asked.

Red Dog only laughed, turning away from the bristling Pinkerton agent who glared at him with scornful black eyes.

CHAPTER SEVENTEEN

Red Dog put Raider, Thalia, and Wilson in the storm cellar of the ranch house. Wilson was still unconscious and suffering from the wound on his shoulder. Raider wasn't sure if he would live or die. He had seen men recover from worse and pass on from less.

Thalia held her husband's head in her lap, stroking his hair in the cool darkness of the enclosure. "Is he going to die, Ray?"

Raider hovered over Wilson, trying to see the wound. "I wish it was daylight in here."

Thalia pointed to the stone basement wall. "There's a lamp over there. Some matches too."

Raider lit the lamp and turned up the flame. He waved the light over the bloody gash in the rancher's shoulder. Thalia also looked, but then had to turn away.

"It ain't that bad," Raider said. "Has he got a fever?"

Thalia felt her husband's forehead. "No."

Raider touched the wound, feeling beneath the muscle for the bone. "The slug musta grazed him on top o' his shoulder," he told her. "The bone ain't broken. We gotta help that wound, though."

"I'll tear a bandage from the hem of my dress," Thalia offered.

Raider felt his throat closing up, choking back tears. "You always was quick t' help out."

Thalia's cold eyes fixed on the big man's face. "Don't love me, Raider. I won't allow it. I love Mac. You tried to prove he did wrong . . ."

"And *I* was wrong, Thalia. Not Mac."

She lowered his eyes. "I suspected he was having trouble.

163

We owe a loan at a bank in Billings. When the note comes due, we're gonna lose Three Forks."

"I'm sorry."

Thalia seemed to soften in an instant, putting her hand on Raider's forearm. "You misinterpreted the facts, Ray. It could have happened to anyone. I was listening at the window upstairs. You had *me* believing you for a minute."

Raider looked down at Wilson. "We gotta fix that hole in your boy there. Is there any liniment down here? Or any gunpowder?"

"There's a jug of corn squeezin's."

Raider gave her a half smile. "Whose idea was that?"

"Mac likes to have a nip now and then."

"I bet I'd like 'im if he wasn't in such a snit," Raider said.

Thalia smiled. "I bet you would too."

With Thalia directing him, Raider found the jug of moonshine. He poured it on the wound, dousing the bloody tissue. When it was soaked good, he struck a match and lit the wound. Wilson flinched as it burned. Raider let it go for a couple of seconds and then patted it out.

Wilson opened his eyes. "What was that?"

"Red Dog shot you, pardner," Raider said.

Thalia kissed his forehead. "Be quiet, Mac. You're hurt."

Wilson looked up at Raider, his eyes pleading. "Didn't know about Red Dog, that he had my men. Swear it."

"It's okay," Raider said. "I heard 'em talkin' while they was bringin' us here. Said they agreed t' work for Red Dog only if he would leave you alone. They were hittin' Cantrell's place, then drivin' the cattle all around to make it look like both sides were gettin' hit. In the meantime, you an' Cantrell was blamin' each other. Red Dog plans t' take advantage o' the range war t' fleece all the stolen cattle he can get his hands on. Gonna drive 'em north an' sell 'em t' the Canadian Injuns."

Thalia squinted at the big man. "How did you know all that?"

Raider shrugged. "Kept my ears open while they was draggin' us down into this cellar."

"Corn squeezin's," Wilson said faintly.

Raider gave him a long pull from the bottle. Wilson swallowed and put his head in Thalia's lap. He muttered something that sounded like a thank you to Raider, then closed his eyes and went back to sleep.

Raider and Thalia were silent.

After a while, Raider started to look for a way out. But there was only one door, the hatch directly above them. And that was locked from the outside.

"Is Red Dog really gonna hang us?" Thalia asked.

Raider tried to look reassuring. "Well, he ain't done it yet."

They sat for a long time before they heard the clattering above them. Was Red Dog coming for them before dawn? Maybe he couldn't wait to string them up.

"Pinkerton! Are you there?"

The voice was a hoarse whisper that Raider recognized immediately. "Rich Elk! I forgot all 'bout 'im. Hey, boy, how you doin'? See if you can get us the hell outta here."

"There's a lock," the half-breed replied. "I will get some tools and set you free."

Raider listened as he hurried off. "We might have a chance yet."

Thalia looked doubtful. "How will we get away from Red Dog and his men? Mac can't ride."

"You'd be s'prised what somebody can do when their life is on the line, honey. Let's just take it one step at a time. Or would you rather wait round for Red Dog's necktie party?"

"One step at a time," Thalia replied, a dainty hand to her throat.

It seemed like forever before they heard the clattering on the storm door. Raider called to Rich Elk, but the only reply was the sound of a file on a metal lock. The half-breed was actually going to spring them.

He could hear the doors rattling. "Almost there."

When they swung open, Raider started to stand up. Something fell, brushing him, knocking him back onto the dirt floor of the cellar. Thalia screamed. Someone laughed above them.

Raider looked over at the fallen body of Rich Elk, whose neck had been sliced from ear to ear.

Red Dog thought his handiwork to be amusing. "He will never stop smiling now. Even if he was your last chance!"

The evil laughter rolled over the barnyard.

One of Red Dog's men closed the storm door.

"How can Mac's own hands help that madman?" Thalia said.

Raider exhaled, sighing deeply. "Mac knows what's goin' on now. It's their butts if somebody points the finger. Although, with the marshal lyin' dead out there, there ain't much law in these parts."

Raider looked at the body of Rich Elk. "I better cover 'im up with somethin'." He found a couple of burlap sacks and draped them over the corpse.

Thalia started to cry, sobbing quietly, tears pouring down her face.

Wilson coughed until Raider gave him some more of the corn liquor.

He took another slug himself and sat silently, waiting for the dawn.

Since there weren't many trees on Three Forks, Red Dog decided to hang them in the barn.

They were led to the stable, where ropes were hanging from the rafters. Raider was placed on the mule that had been the last mount for Shorty Jenkins. Thalia and her husband stood together, looking pitiful. Wilson could walk now, but he was still weak.

"I've never hung a white man before," Red Dog announced to his men.

There were five hands left after the damage Raider had done. The hands didn't seem as eager to hang anybody. They knew they had to go along, having chosen the dark path with Red Dog, but they weren't enthusiastic about it.

Thalia peered up at Raider. "You sure Bobby is all right, Ray?"

She had asked him the same question a hundred times during the night.

Raider nodded. "He's safe. Even this Apache bastard can't get 'is hands on 'im."

Red Dog frowned. "You talk mighty smart for a man who's about to have a rope around his neck."

"Kiss my ass, you peckerwood Injun. I'd sooner die a hundred times before I'd give you the pleasure o' seein' me afraid. Do your worst. It won't be the first time some *pisto-lero* tried t' kill me."

Red Dog grinned hideously. "No, but it will be the first time somebody *succeeded* in killing you."

Raider glared right back at him. "Cut my hands loose, you chicken-shit renegade. I'll fight you man t' man an' carve you a new gizzard."

Red Dog waved his arm. "Put the noose around his neck."

One of the hands led the mule under the first rope. Raider counted the loops on the knot—thirteen. At least it was a good knot, one that would break his neck, get it over with quick. He wouldn't have to hang there and strangle like he had seen at some lynchings.

Red Dog's man tightened the noose. Then he looked over at Wilson. "Sorry about this, Mr. Mac. I wish it didn't have to be this way. We woulda probably stayed with you if you coulda paid us."

Wilson stiffened next to his wife. "Ain't no call to go bad, Eban. You coulda signed on with Cantrell. I woulda felt better about that than seein' you ride with the likes of this scum."

Red Dog pointed at Wilson. "The woman is next."

Wilson made a move but the pain in his shoulder got him.

Raider had his eyes closed, anticipating death. He felt bad for Wilson. Red Dog was going to make him watch Thalia die first. At least the big man from Arkansas would not have to see that.

"Hang him!" Red Dog cried.

The Apache raised his hand to slap the mule.

Raider heard the crack, felt the animal riding out from under him.

He expected the rope to tighten, his stomach rising as he fell.

A loud burst from a scattergun roared through the stable. Raider hit the floor of the barn, landing with a thud, losing his breath, but still alive with his neck in one piece. Then there were men running around, shooting and raising hell.

Raider looked up to see Red Dog grabbing Thalia.

"No!"

The Apache jumped onto the mule and rode out of the barn, charging through the yard to the west.

Johnny Dallas ran up next to Raider and aimed his Colt at the fleeing renegade.

"Don't shoot!" Raider cried. "He's got the woman with 'im!"

Dallas lowered the Peacemaker. "Well don't thank me for savin' your bacon, Pinkerton."

"Was that you with the shotgun, blastin' my hang rope?"

Dallas nodded. He reached down and cut Raider's bonds. The big man stood up, rubbing his wrists.

Asa Cantrell cantered up on a mare. "Our boys got the five that was workin' for Red Dog and Wilson." He gestured to the rancher, who had passed out.

Raider shook his head. "Wilson wasn't in on it."

Cantrell looked dubious. "S'pose you tell me how you know that."

"No time." He pointed west. "Red Dog grabbed the woman. I gotta go after 'im."

"I'm goin' too," Dallas offered.

Raider grimaced at the gunslinger. "Thought you was interested in stayin' alive, Dallas."

The gunslinger smiled. "You get in trouble if you're left alone, big man. I got to come along to see that you don't get yourself killed."

"I ain't got time t' argue," Raider replied. "Let's find a couplea fast horses and get to it."

Cantrell clapped his hands and called behind him. Several of his crewmen were tying up Red Dog's gang. They gave up their mounts to Raider and Dallas. Cantrell also gave Raider his Winchester and a couple of sticks of dynamite.

"You know how the red stuff works?" Cantrell asked.

Raider tucked the dynamite in his shirt. "Red thunder and I are old friends, Asa. What made you think t' bring it?"

"Didn't know what manner of trouble we'd find here," Cantrell replied. "I like to be ready for anything."

Raider swung into the saddle of a big black gelding.

Dallas jumped onto a bay mare.

"Good luck, boys," Cantrell said.

Raider started forward, but then reined up and looked back at the red-haired rancher. "You let me go when you knew I was a Pink."

Cantrell nodded. "Figured if anybody could get the job done, it would be you. Had no choice but to free you."

"How'd you know t' come here?" Raider asked. "How'd you know I was movin' on Three Forks?"

"The boy," Cantrell replied. "He stole Tinker's pack mule and rode to tell me. We came in at dawn to surprise Wilson. Didn't know we'd be findin' Red Dog too."

Raider glanced down at the rancher. "Take care o' Wilson. I'll be back when I get that renegade."

He spurred the black out of the stable, with the dapper gunslinger's mare following in his tracks.

As he rode west, he realized that the boy had saved his life. He had to be proud of Bobby Wilson. Thank God the kid was safe and sound.

CHAPTER EIGHTEEN

Bobby Wilson felt pretty proud of himself for going to tell Cantrell that Raider was riding into Three Forks with only the marshal to back him up. Bobby had been partially concerned with Raider's welfare, but he had been more interested in making sure his father wasn't hurt. He had been afraid at first to face Cantrell, but after they came eye to eye, he was able to convince the red-haired rancher to at least take his crew and have a look at Three Forks.

Cantrell and his men had left before dawn, while Bobby was sleeping. When he woke, he felt cheated that he had not been able to go along. So he went to the remuda and got himself a gentle filly to ride north. He kept a steady pace until he saw a rider coming. Or was it two riders? A man and a woman were riding the same horse.

Bobby waved and the rider turned toward him. Good. Maybe the man would have news from Three Forks. He was dying to hear what had happened.

He spurred the filly into a lope, heading for the rider.

He hoped his father and mother were safe.

The rider would be able to tell him.

Bobby reined up when he got close enough to see the Indian.

His stomach turned when he saw his mother riding in front of Red Dog.

He wanted to cry.

The Indian drew a pistol and Bobby stared down the dark-eyed bore of certain death.

Raider followed Red Dog's tracks until they converged with the hoofprints of another mount.

He reined up and got down to study the tracks. "Red Dog met somebody an' took off with 'em t' the southwest."

Dallas tipped back his Stetson. "Maybe the tracks just cross. Maybe he didn't meet anybody."

Raider shook his head. "Nope, look here. They approached each other from different directions, then met up an' rode off t'gether."

"Don't know much about trackin'," Dallas replied. "I just know about shootin'. Get me near that Injun and I'll blow him to kingdom come."

Raider started to mount up, but something caught his eye. He reached down to pick up a lump of metal in the dirt. It was an old pistol, all rust and dirt. The same one he had seen before. The kid must have rescued it from the scrap heap at Three Forks. It had been his most prized possession.

Raider looked to the southwest. "He's got the boy."

"Bobby Wilson?"

"Yep."

Dallas frowned. "How do you know that? The kid is safe at Delta Plain."

"I'll explain when we find 'im," Raider said.

Until then, there was only time to ride.

They followed the tracks to the rocky ridge, where they ended. Raider looked north, along the ridge. He knew where Red Dog was going. He told Dallas about the box canyon and the hidden herd.

Dallas nodded, looking sideways at him.

Raider squinted back at the gunman. "What?"

"There were bodies strewed all over Three Forks," the gunslinger replied. "Did you do that?"

Raider lowered his eyes. "I did most of it. Though I can't say I'm proud o' all that killin'. Even if it was needed."

Dallas tipped his hat. "Proud to be ridin' with you, partner. Let's go get the Injun."

Raider glared at the shootist. "Nothin' happens t' the boy or the woman. We wait for a clear shot on Red Dog. Understood?"

Dallas nodded.

They spurred north, following the ridge.

Raider reined up before he got to the entrance to Red Dog's hideout.

"Ain't we goin' in?" Dallas asked.

"No. We wait for it t' get dark."

Dallas sighed. "I don't reckon I have to tell you what that buck will do to that boy and that woman?"

Raider snapped at the gunslinger. "No! You don't haveta tell me. You just haveta keep your goddamn mouth shut until it gets dark."

Dallas knew better than to ask any questions, but he figured Raider's temper had something to do with the woman and the kid. Without further comment he guided his mount into the rocks and climbed out of the saddle.

Raider dismounted as well. "Sorry, Dallas. I'm a little edgy. I went after that redskin with Weeks an' Martin. You saw what happened t' both o' them."

Dallas chortled, shaking his head. "That buck's got a thing for slicin' throats, don't he? Give me a head-on gunfight any day."

"Savages ain't like you an' me. They ain't God-fearin'."

Dallas frowned. "Yeah, you and me is real God-fearin' all right."

Raider figured the shootist had a right to be sarcastic, but he still considered himself and the gunman above men like Red Dog.

"Who dies for the sins of the gunslinger?" Dallas asked. "Tell me that, Pinkerton."

"All the men he killed," Raider replied. "I reckon that would be enough."

Dallas laughed and reached into his saddlebag. He took out a bundle that was wrapped in cloth. "I been savin' this, Ray. Somebody give it to me, only I can't bring myself to use it. I guess I'm just too attached to this Peacemaker on my hip. Best that you take it."

He handed the bundle to Raider, who unrolled the cloth to find a mint-condition '73 Colt. "Wooden handles," the big man said. "Whoever give you this gun knew what you like."

"Take it," Dallas said. "I got a feelin' you're gonna need it."

They sat in the rocks, waiting for it to get dark.

"You really think Red Dog is with those stolen cows?" Dallas asked the big man.

"That mule wouldn't get him much further," Raider replied. "Besides, he ain't leavin' what he's worked so hard for."

"I sure hope you're right."

Raider figured his mistake with Weeks and Martin had been leaving them by themselves. They should have come along, backing him up. At least he could have kept an eye on them. When he went into the canyon this time, he was taking the gunslinger with him.

"Are we close yet?" asked Johnny Dallas.

Raider told him to hush.

They had been making their way through the rocks for the better part of two hours. Raider kept listening, expecting the wild-eyed Apache to burst out of the shadows with hot iron in hand. Raider wouldn't have minded taking Red Dog like that. At least if the Indian made the first move, Thalia and the kid would be safe.

Raider wondered if the boy had inherited his penchant for getting into trouble, for riding headlong into the mouth of misfortune. How else could Bobby have managed to get captured by the Apache? Maybe the gun had been thrown there by someone else. Raider knew better. It had been a signal. The boy was smart enough to do that.

Dallas drew closer to him in the shadows, speaking in a raspy whisper. "What if he ain't down there? I mean, he ain't crazy enough to think he can drive those cows by hisself."

"Just keep movin'," the big man replied. "We'll be there soon enough. Then you can decide for yourself if Red Dog is around."

Raider started forward. Dallas put a hand on his shoulder. "I don't like this, Ray. Maybe I ought to circle around, come in from a different angle."

Raider did not feel like arguing. "Suit yourself. Just be quiet. If you see something, come an' find me."

"And if I have to shoot before I find you?"

"Nothin' happens to the woman or the boy," Raider replied. "Remember that."

Dallas nodded and moved off to his left.

Raider wondered if it was a mistake to have brought along the gunslinger. Dallas might be good in a showdown, but Red Dog wasn't the kind to face you and draw fair. He couldn't worry about it. He just moved again, heading through the shadows toward the box canyon.

Raider looked down into the hidden canyon. The cows were still there. Their horns clicked as they moved restlessly in the dark. Even after Raider had let some of them go, Red Dog had managed to get them back into the canyon. He had also added a few head to the herd.

Leaning on the edge of the canyon, Raider looked down the barrel of Cantrell's Winchester. He had not taken the time to ask about the gun's particulars, if it shot high or low, left or right. He also took the new Colt from his belt, laying it next to him on the rock ledge.

This time, Raider intended to wait for the Apache.

For a long while, he sat motionless. His eyes and ears were alert for sounds of movement. When he heard the mule braying, he knew that Red Dog was down there somewhere. He tried not to think about the two unfortunate souls Red Dog had with him.

He expected to hear Thalia crying out during the night, but he was encouraged when he didn't. Maybe Red Dog had abandoned them somewhere. Then again, maybe he had killed them.

No sounds through the night, except the mule and the cattle.

Raider thought he heard a short scream, the throttling cry of a man. But he opened his eyes and figured he had fallen asleep, dreaming the weird cry. He looked to the heavens to see a purple glow appearing in the east. Almost dawn. He thought about Johnny Dallas, wondering if the gunslinger was all right. When the sun was high enough, he got his answer.

Red Dog had killed the shootist. Dallas was strung from the rim of the canyon, naked, dangling by his legs. Red Dog had gotten him during the night. Raider hadn't dreamed the man's scream after all.

"That son of a bitch."

Then he heard singing, the off-key lilt of a savage voice.

Looking down into the canyon, he saw Red Dog staggering into the herd. He was drinking from a whiskey bottle and seemed to be carrying something on his side. Raider aimed the rifle, until he realized that Thalia was hanging onto Red Dog as the Indian dragged her among the steers.

No way he could risk a shot.

Red Dog walked to the gate that restrained the cattle. He opened the gate and urged the steers onto the trail. His laughter was drunken and hateful. Raider wanted to get off a shot. But Thalia was there, as if the Indian knew she would be good cover.

Then the boy staggered out of the rocks. He was bloody and bruised. Raider didn't even want to think about what Red Dog had done to the kid. Sitting at the rim of the canyon, Raider felt stupid and helpless. He watched as Bobby got up his strength enough to rush straight at Red Dog.

Raider aimed, close to firing. Thalia was there. If he could just hit Red Dog in the head.

Bobby charged but the Indian knocked him away like a grizzly swatting a ground squirrel. The kid squirmed on the ground. Raider had to do something. He grabbed Dallas's Colt and stood up on the ledge.

"Bobby!"

Red Dog turned to fire at him with a pistol.

Raider launched the Colt into the air, trying to throw it toward the boy. Red Dog's shots fell short. The Colt landed at the Apache's feet.

Red Dog laughed and kicked the gun toward Bobby. "Go on," he sneered. "Let me see if you got the guts. Draw, cowboy."

Red Dog laughed like a madman.

Bobby was staring at the gun.

Raider aimed the Winchester, figuring it was do or die, hoping he would not hit Thalia.

"Go on," Red Dog urged again. "Shoot me if you can."

Raider fired a shot that went over Red Dog's head.

That was enough, though. The Indian flinched, taking his eyes off the boy. That was all Bobby needed. He picked up the Colt and fired until the chambers were empty.

"Yeah!" Raider cried. "Kill that son of a bitch."

Red Dog let go of Thalia, dropping her to the ground. He staggered forward, like he could not believe he had been shot. Bobby threw the Colt into his chest.

"You shot me!" the Apache cried. "Nobody ever shot me before."

Raider fired the Winchester, slamming two slugs into the Indian's skull. Red Dog fell on his face, twitching in the dust. Bobby ran to the body and started to kick the dead renegade. He didn't quit until Raider climbed down and stopped him.

"It's all right," he told the boy with black eyes. "He ain't gonna hurt you no more."

The kid buried his face in Raider's chest, sobbing.

Raider held him for a moment and then said, "Let's go tend to your ma."

"Okay, Paw," the boy replied.

At first, Raider thought the kid knew. But then he realized that Bobby had deliriously mistaken him for Mac Wilson. He led the boy to the spot where Thalia was lying. They knelt beside her.

Raider lifted her head. "Are you all right?" he asked.

"No," she replied. "But I reckon I'll live."

She touched her boy's hand.

Bobby began to cry.

After a moment, Raider realized he was crying too.

CHAPTER NINETEEN

A week after Raider brought Thalia and Bobby back to Three Forks, he was sitting on the front porch with Mac Wilson, looking out over the spread. Wilson had his arm in a sling, relieving some of the pressure on his wounded shoulder. Red Dog's Sharps had taken quite a bite out of him.

"How's the wing?" Raider asked.

Mac Wilson nodded, his eyes blank. "It'll be all right," he replied with the voice of a defeated man. He looked at Raider. "Where you been this week? You skeedaddled and didn't give me a chance to thank you for gettin' Thalia and the boy."

Raider gazed out toward the shimmering Montana plain. "I was endin' it once an' for all," the big man replied. "An' you don't have t' thank me. Just hear me out on a few things."

Wilson said he would, but not before they had a slug of corn whiskey.

Raider obliged the rancher, drinking a long pull from the jug and wiping his mouth with the back of his hand. "Smooth. You make that yourself?"

Wilson nodded. "Rich Elk taught me how."

For a moment, they were silent, remembering all that had happened, all the men who had died. There hadn't really been any reason for it, except Red Dog's meanness. But when Raider thought hard on it, he knew that no bad thing ever happened for a good reason.

"How's the boy doin'?" Raider asked.

"He's talkin' now. Went out to ride today. First time he's been out of the house since you brought him back. Been kinda quiet around here."

Raider wanted to ask about Thalia, but he didn't want to offend Wilson.

The rancher seemed to know his thoughts. "She's okay. Still skittish. I suspect she will be for a while. The buffalo old come from Cantrell's and doctored her. Thalia is a tough woman. She'll come through. She always has."

"Good," was all the big man said.

Wilson put the jug next to his chair. "Well, you said you wanted me to hear you out. Let's have it."

Raider didn't have to tell him about his own particulars— sending the wire from Billings, visiting the territorial marshal to tell him about Mays, writing a report and posting it back to Chicago.

He had come to help Wilson, if the rancher would let him. Men could be proud about things. Too much sometimes. They could lose everything to pride. Raider had seen it before.

"I know you like t' come to a point," he said to Wilson, "so I'll just say my piece. You owe the bank in Billings come September."

Wilson flinched. "That ain't none of your lookout."

Raider tipped back his Stetson. "You said you'd hear me out. I take it that you are a man of your word."

"I am that."

"Then listen t' me."

Wilson said he would listen without interrupting, but that he was not one to accept charity.

Raider took a deep breath and started in. "A man ain't nothin' if he can't take a helpin' hand once in a while. There's two sides t' charity, give an' receive. I'm sayin' you should be one t' receive, Wilson. Otherwise that boy an' Thalia won't have no one t' depend on. Just cause you're a leg down, don't mean you can't lift yourself up."

Wilson chortled. "You sound like a preacher."

"Well, maybe you need t' be preached at," Raider replied. "Otherwise, you'll be scoffin' at a way outta your troubles."

Wilson reached for the jug. "All right, mister miracle man, tell me what it'll take to turn Three Forks around."

Raider leaned forward. "When I was at Cantrell's a while back, one o' his men told me they was turnin' back your cattle when they brought them in with the Delta Plain herd."

"So?"

Raider laughed. "*So* this. I took the liberty o' tellin' Cantrell t' round up your cows when he made the final sweep through the hill country. Seems Red Dog had a couplea herds stashed away an' a bunch of 'em was your cows. Cantrell's boys brought in a few more, so it ain't lookin' so bad if you can get them t' market."

Wilson lowered his head. "How am I gonna drive a bunch of steers south without any cowboys? And my arm in a sling."

"That's the best part," Raider replied. "You don't haveta go. Cantrell agreed t' hire extra hands an' pay them out o' your share at the end o' the trail drive."

Wilson perked up. "That's fair. Hey, how many head does Cantrell figure I got, anyway?"

"He got about eight hundred head now, and he figgers there'll be a hundred or so on the last sweep."

Wilson could not believe it. "How'd I end up with that many?"

"Red Dog hit you first, in the spring when all this started. You thought your cows had died, but they were west o' here an' in that canyon."

Wilson sighed. "I don't know if I can take charity from a man like Cantrell. I just don't know."

"Can't you see?" Raider pleaded. "The man is tryin' to make up for all the trouble. Hell, didn't he save your ass from Red Dog?"

"Saved yourn too!" Wilson replied.

Raider laughed. "That he did, Mac. That he did."

Wilson laughed but then fell back into his misery. "Cantrell's idea might work. But how'm I supposed to get us through until September? I'm dead busted."

"Cantrell can bring you a few beef steers, and you can still plant a squash garden, maybe some corn. There's game if you can hunt. Maybe you can get credit from Tinker."

"I got creditors in Ekalaka. They won't even sell me a piss pot if I don't pay up. An' Tinker don't give credit to no one."

Raider sighed, shaking his head. "You're a hard man, Mac Wilson. You leave me no choice but t' shoot you."

Wilson looked sideways at him. "You ain't gonna shoot me!"

"No, but it'd hurt you about as bad as what I'm gonna ask o' you next. Here. Take this."

Raider held out a leather pouch.

Wilson looked away. "I ain't takin' your money."

"It ain't mine," Raider replied, knowing that some of it was his back pay. "There was a reward for Red Dog. Since Pinks ain't allowed t' take rewards, I got it for Bobby."

Wilson turned quickly to glare at him. "I ain't . . ."

"Bobby shot Red Dog, Mac."

The rancher gawked at him. "Bobby?"

"He didn't tell you, huh?"

"No. I reckon he didn't want to."

Raider explained the way Bobby had learned to shoot, the way he was a natural with a gun. "The way I see it," the big man said, "this money is yours. It belongs to your family. There's four hundred dollars there."

"Four hundred!"

"Red Dog was a wanted man."

Raider left out the part about including most of his back wages and some money he found in Red Dog's hideout when he went to search for his things. He had also retrieved his saddle, his rifle and his saddlebags. His boots and good Stetson had not turned up, but he had found his roan stallion.

Wilson's eyes sparkled for the first time since the shooting. "Bobby shot Red Dog. I'll be."

"Do I hear two gentlemen on my front porch?"

Thalia Wilson glided onto the porch with her white dress flowing all around her. She looked like an angel, Raider thought. Her skin was drawn and some of the bruises had not yet healed. But she was strong and with a good man like Wilson to help her, she'd make it back to full strength.

"I'm so glad you came, Ray," she said softly. "Bobby was so afraid he wouldn't get to say good-bye to you."

Raider blushed. "I thought I'd go without sayin' so long t' Bobby. It might make him think of unpleasant things."

"Like what?" Thalia asked.

Raider squinted at her. "Thalia . . ."

"She don't remember a thing," Wilson said quickly.

Raider felt uncomfortable. "Oh, I . . . well, maybe that's for the best."

"Look," Thalia said, "Bobby is comin'."

Bobby Wilson galloped toward the porch on his sorrel

gelding. He reined up when he saw Raider. He waved and eased the sorrel into a walk.

"Ray. Howdy!"

Raider tipped his hat.

Thalia looked up at her son. "Bobby, I told you about ridin' so close to the house. That dust."

"Sorry, Maw." The boy's black eyes were glowing. "Ray, you gonna stay for dinner?"

The big man from Arkansas smiled weakly. "Uh, no, Bobby. I can't stay tonight. I gotta be on my way."

"Shoot," the young man replied.

Thalia sat down next to her husband. "Bobby, why don't you ride with Ray to the edge of the ranch? Wouldn't you like that, Mr. Howard?"

Raider wondered for a moment if Thalia remembered the truth about Bobby. About Raider being his real father. But then he saw the nod, the gleam in her eye. She figured it was more important for him to say good-bye to the boy than to her.

"Sure," Bobby said. "Ray, I'll ride with you. You wouldn't mind, would you?"

Raider shook his head. "No, I wouldn't mind. If your paw says it's okay."

Bobby looked at Mac Wilson, who nodded. "You ride with him, Ray. And you come back here anytime," Wilson said. "I'll never forget what you done for me. I reckon it sort of squares things all the way around."

Bobby got Raider's roan and led it to the porch.

Raider swung into the saddle. "So long, Thalia."

She tried her best to smile, although tears were streaming down her cheeks. "Get out of here, you black-eyed cowboy. And try not to get yourself killed."

Raider turned the roan and rode away without looking back.

The boy followed him for a long time before Raider reined up and turned to regard him. "D'you remember killin' Red Dog?" Raider asked.

Bobby frowned. He had not expected such a question. Raider repeated it for him. Bobby said that he did remember.

"D'you remember how it felt?" Raider asked.

Bobby thought about it and then replied, "It felt bad. I knew I had to do it, but it still felt bad."

Raider nodded. "That's how it oughtta feel. I want you t' promise me you won't never kill again unless you have to."

"I promise." The boy was starting to cry, although he did not know why the tears were coming. "I promise, damn you!"

Raider reached back for his saddlebag. "I want you t' have somethin'. That gunslinger gave it to me. Your maw would hang me if she knowed I was . . . well, here, just take it."

He threw the '73 Colt to the boy.

Bobby looked at it, still crying. "Why are you giving this to me?"

"Because a man needs a gun in these parts," Raider replied. "But that still don't mean it's right t' kill."

The boy was hurting. "Was it a sin to kill Red Dog?" he asked. "Please tell me, Ray."

Raider took off his hat, wiping his brow with the back of his forearm. He looked up at the sky. "Well, I don't think killin' Red Dog will keep you out o' heaven, Bobby. Though it wouldn't hurt t' ask forgiveness."

"I have, Ray. I really have."

"So long, son. You help your ma and pa, you hear?"

"I will. Thanks for the gun . . ."

But Raider had already turned the stallion, heading west for Billings, where he would pick up his next assignment from the Pinkerton agency.

Bobby guided the sorrel toward Three Forks. He did not look back. He did not see Raider when he reined up for a moment, stopping to take one more glimpse of the boy who rode away from him.

EPILOGUE

Raider rode toward a light in the distance. He hoped it was the cantina he had been searching for. He knew it was somewhere near the Oklahoma–Texas border. All he wanted was a meal, a shot of whiskey, and a night's sleep. Not too much to ask for a man who had just put Jimbo Weathers in the ground. The people of the Oklahoma panhandle would sleep better without Weathers to ride hell-bent into their nightly dreams.

The sheriff in Norman wanted the body brought back, but he would have to do with Weathers' possessions as proof. The Buntline with the notches in the butt would be convincing. Nobody could have gotten the Buntline away from Weathers while he was alive. Raider knew, because he had tried.

It was the cantina on the horizon.

Raider knew it was near the railroad tracks. He would sell the roan if he could and catch the train. Ordinarily he hated riding in a day coach, but he felt tired in the saddle. Maybe he just needed something to perk him up. Sleep would be a big help.

He tied the roan at the hitching post and checked his Colt. He wanted to be ready if anyone gave him a try. He had been in the cantina before, but that was no reason to think the proprietor would remember him. And there was always the chance that he would cross paths with a former adversary.

He pushed through the door.

"Ray! You big Pinkerton galoot!"

His hand paused on its way to the Peacemaker. Did he remember the voice? It was a friendly female tone.

Bright Feather stepped out of the shadows. "Ray. Remember me? From all that trouble two months back in Montana!"

Raider gaped at the Cheyenne girl who had run away from her preacher husband and, apparently, Asa Cantrell. "Hell, girl, how'd you end up down here in Oklahoma?"

She put a finger to her lips. "Shh, José is sleepin'. Let's go out back. There's a stable and a tub. I'll give you a bath."

Raider went with her. He stripped and eased down into a cold tub. It felt icy until she started to rub him with soap.

"Your pecker is swellin'," Bright Feather said, reaching into the tub to fondle him.

Raider tried to pull her in with him.

"Not just yet," she said. "I gotta tell you all the news."

She was full of gossip. Cantrell's cattle drive had turned out fine. He had come back to Three Forks to give Mac Wilson twice the money he needed to settle his note at the bank. Then Cantrell offered to buy out Wilson and Wilson turned around and accepted the offer. Wilson took Thalia and Bobby east, settling in Chicago where it was rumored that he had used the money to get into the livestock trade. Thalia was living in a big house near the lake and Bobby was in a proper school.

Raider had to smile at that. Thalia and Bobby in Chicago, walking the same streets as Wagner and Pinkerton. What would his distinguished bosses say if they knew Raider's son was living right under their noses?

"Life sure deals funny cards sometimes," he said to Bright Feather. "What 'bout that sister o' yours?"

"Oh, she married Cantrell. She's expecting a little red-haired half-breed come late winter, early spring."

Raider nodded. "And what 'bout you, Bright Feather?"

The girl poured a bucket of cold water over his head. "I'm a whore, Raider. I done accepted that about myself. My ass is hot but my heart is cold. I ain't meant for nothin' more than what I'm doin'. I guess I'm just a Cheyenne chippy. Maybe it was all that religion that done it."

Raider shook the water out of his hair. "I ain't one to bad mouth religion, but I could see where it might get . . ."

She doused him with another pail of water.

Raider tried to grab her, to pull her into the tub.

Bright Feather laughed and ran for the stable in back.

Raider climbed out of the tub, grabbed his guns, and chased after her.

She fell into the straw, spreading her legs. "I never thought I'd see you, big man. Hell, all we ever get in here are dumb Mexicans and cowboys. I never enjoy it when they're pokin' me, but I take the money."

"I ain't sure I have any money," Raider teased.

She reached up and grabbed his cock. "No charge, cowboy. Not for you. Now give me that big thing."

Raider slipped down beside her. He leaned on one arm for a minute, looking down at her. Smooth dark skin, thick lips, proud nose, coarse black hair. He would have given every dime he had to lie beside her.

"What's wrong with you?" she said, teasing him.

He touched her cheek. "I was just thinkin' how beautiful you are."

"Show me," she said, lifting her face to kiss him. "Show me how beautiful you think I am."

He wanted to take it slow, to enjoy it.

But after a few minutes, they lost control and began to writhe with pleasure on the rustling straw.